Lady of
Leighton Manor

For:
Celecia

With special thanks to Anna & Bobbie

Copyright April 2015

B. E. Brown

Acknowledgments

I have been blessed with a wonderful support system and cheerleaders on my writing. First and foremost, my amazing husband Travis Brown who has always been supportive and encouraging even when writing took long hours and sleepless nights. My mother and father, Lyman & Beth Sibbett, who instilled a deep love of the written word in me as a small child and have always been my first editors, I would have never been able to realize the dream of writing a book without their help and love.

I'd also like to say "thank you" to those people that inspire my work, acted as sounding boards, inspired characters, book covers, story lines, and have been a large part of the process in countless ways!

Celecia Gallagher and Anna Sibbett who acted as my first string editors and story consultants, without whom this book wouldn't have been possible.

Thank you, Celecia for writing the story synopsis and for putting up with my *numerous* texts and phone calls regarding story ideas and writers block! Thank you, Anna for composing the beautiful piano arrangement that I have been given the honor of printing along side my book, as well as pushing me to improve the story at every turn.

My deepest thanks to Bobbie Brown, for all your time and energy spent doing the final edit on this book as well as creating its cover. As always it was such a joy to work with you and I look forward to many more chances to do so again in the future.

My gratitude is also extended to Lori Ann Sibbett for your endless encouragement with this project.

Thank you, you have all been instrumental in my process.

~Prologue~

LaVet glowered at her older brother and gritted her teeth gripping the branch tighter between her slender hands.

"Again." Barton commanded and took up a defensive stance, holding his own branch at the ready.

She took a wild, angry swing at him. It was easily deflected and Barton laughed loudly. The sound made LaVet seethe and she swung at him again, this time with concentration and forced Barton to defend himself. LaVet advanced, forcing Barton to give ground.

After getting over his surprise at her fury Barton knocked the branch from her hand. "That was better."

"Why? Why must I learn how to fight with a sword?" LaVet panted.

"All women should know how to defend themselves."

"I am a lady. Shouldn't I have a husband to defend me?" LaVet argued.

"You are a lady, and one day you may well have a husband, but every lady should also know how to use a sword and ride a horse. You never know when it could be called for."

"If father knew you were teaching her how to ride and swing a sword like a man, he would be very angry." Octavia said from behind them. She turned to look up at her sister. Dressed in the finest, her golden hair pinned in a very attractive manner, Octavia looked years older than the sixteen she was.

"It's a good thing father doesn't know then isn't it?" Barton said, raising one eyebrow and casting Octavia a smile.

"Come on Little Bit, it's time to get you cleaned up. Father will be back soon and we can't risk him seeing you in this state." Octavia held out one delicate hand for LaVet to take. Dropping the branch LaVet gladly took it and followed Octavia without a backward glance at her brother.

Roche Manor was alight with activity. Aromas from the kitchen wafted through the air and made LaVet's mouth water. Every curtain was drawn back, soft summer light spilling into the rooms and corridors. Maids dusted, mopped and polished every surface.

Octavia pulled LaVet behind her until they reached her chambers and promptly made the younger girl undress and bathe. The two maids attending to her fussed over the amount of dirt under her fingernails and the sad state of her hair, and scrubbed her until her skin felt as though it would fall off.

LaVet was dried and dressed when her mother entered the room. At the sight of her the maids curtseyed low and Octavia rushed to her side, the two exchanging a kiss. The mistress of Roche Manor beamed at her oldest child, "My love, how well you look today."

"Thank you mother," Octavia smiled. "You look beautiful as always." LaVet felt as though she was looking at a mirror image. Her mother and sister were the same height, both with piercing blue eyes, golden hair that shimmered in the light, full red lips and rosy cheeks that always held a hint of a blush. Each was perfection in her own right.

LaVet caught her own reflection in the mirror and sighed. Although tall for her twelve years of age she shared little resemblance to her sister or mother. She wasn't unpleasant looking. With striking features that matched her father's she was reminded that one day she would also be quite the beauty. They shared fair skin, a thin nose and wide emerald green eyes. Her crowning physical attribute was the raven hair that hung well past her waist, although from time to time she did wish for a glow in her cheeks and rose-red lips.

Her mother walked to her and gently placed a hand on her shoulder then took in the state of the bath water and frowned. "You've been out with Barton again, haven't you?"

"He insisted." LaVet argued as her mother shook her head.

"I need to talk to your brother. He must find a more appropriate activity for your time together." She touched LaVet's cheek and ran her finger under the small scratch that ran its way over her cheek.

"It's almost time for your father's arrival. Octavia and I will leave you to have your hair attended to."

LaVet nodded, "Yes, mother."

She tried not to pick at her fingernails while the two maids pulled at and twisted her hair into decorative knots and braids. The process took such a long time that LaVet felt as though days had gone by when they stepped back and pronounced they had finished.

"Thank you, it's very lovely." LaVet admired her reflection and did feel as though a transformation had taken place. She wasn't sure what version of herself she liked better; the image of the lady that stared back at her now or the wild creature with a horse and sword.

***

There was great fanfare with her father's return and he greeted each of his children with kindness and warmth. After a large feast was set out in his honor the family gathered around him to listen to tales of his travels for the King. Hours passed in the pleasant company of her happy family before the night grew too late and the children were sent to take their rest.

The next morning LaVet awoke expecting more festivities, but was dismayed to find the manor quite lacking in any kind of joy. Getting dressed quickly, she rushed to Octavia's room and burst in the door.

"What is wrong? What has happened?" she demanded.

Octavia was seated at her desk; still in her nightshirt, hair let loose around her shoulders, her face looking ashen.

"Nothing has happened." LaVet turned sharply to see her mother enter the room. She looked from her mother's forced smile to Octavia, and knit her eyebrows together.

"You are unwell?" she asked Octavia, not believing her mother's protest.

"I am very well, LaVet." Octavia lifted her eyes to meet LaVet's.

"Your sister is just overly excited, that is all." Their mother moved to stand behind Octavia and placed a hand on each shoulder. "She is to be married in a week's time to Lord Stillwell."

"Stillwell?" LaVet said with disbelief.

"Yes, Octavia will be close by, and we will be able to see your sister often." Their mother smiled.

"He is old." LaVet had many reasons to protest the marriage of her sister but blurted out the first thing that came to mind.

"Lord Stillwell isn't old. He is not yet your father's age and Octavia will be well cared for in his household."

LaVet looked at her sister in disbelief. "Octavia... you can't."

"That's enough LaVet! Your sister will be very happy and you will be happy for her." LaVet knew she needed to bite her tongue and did so. Yet, the look exchanged between sisters said more than any words. LaVet felt deep sadness welling up inside for her sister, and longed to express all that was in her heart.

~ Chapter One ~

Seven years later

"When will you leave?" LaVet asked Barton.

"The commission father purchased for me requires I leave in a month's time," Barton answered and tossed his practice sword from hand to hand. "I will distinguish myself as a military man then come home to run the estate, marry and carry on the honorable Roche name in a future generation." LaVet could hear the tones of sarcasm that edged their way into the truth of his statement.

"What will I do without you?" she asked in desperation.

"You survived fine when I went away to school. I imagine that this will be the same. Besides you do have Frances; you are not completely alone." His blue eyes twinkled with humor.

"Frances has become a dear friend," she conceded happily. "I was opposed to a lady's maid when father first insisted, but I am happy to have her now."

"Sweet sister, you are perpetually opposed to almost everything father insists upon." Barton laughed at the truth of this statement and LaVet reached up to tussle his dark hair in a playful gesture.

"I would argue with you, but I so hate being wrong," LaVet said with a pout. "I don't mean to be so difficult. I just don't know how to keep the thoughts that run wild through my mind from bursting out of my mouth."

"It is a problem." Barton agreed, then jumped backward as LaVet took a swing at him, the tip of her practice sword just missing his chest. Then he laughed heartily, "Adding your flare for the dramatic with a bit of anger, I see."

Not willing to continue the conversation, LaVet engaged Barton in a new round of swordplay and for the first time bested him.

"Your technique has greatly improved," he said between deep breaths.

"Yes, one more thing to disappoint father with."

"LaVet, you do know that you are not a disappointment to anyone? Being able to use a sword or ride is nothing to be ashamed of. You have a wildly good eye when it comes to using a gun, and I've never met a better hunter."

"All qualities prized in a *son*. Truly, Barton, you have been my best friend and blessing, yet at the same time I fear that your influence has been a much stronger one on me than that of our mother or sister." LaVet swung the practice sword at her side as they walked toward the house. "I'm afraid that neither of them were around long enough."

"In my dear mother's and Octavia's defense, you didn't have much desire to learn how to sew or embroider pillows, to paint or tend the flowers in the garden…"

LaVet cut him off. "… or sing like a lark or play any instrument at all with any level of proficiency."

"Yet you are lighter on your feet than any other woman I know of. Everyone enjoys the delight of seeing you dance and you are a skillful musician as well. I know for a fact that you also enjoy praise in those other talents already listed."

"Thank you Barton. I guess I am not a lost hope after all," she teased and jabbed him in the ribs with her elbow. "No, not a lost hope to be sure. I have yet to skirt around the edge of impropriety by wearing the wrong colors of dress when visitors come to call or at the wrong time of day, donning Mother's pearls or calling on a man without leaving a card or forbid, taking a ride in a gig alone with a man!" she said and covered her mouth with one hand in mock shock.

"Yes, your reputation as an honorable lady is intact." Barton said laughing.

"Lady LaVet Roche a pillar of female gentility." She did a halfhearted bow. "I will make a great match, no doubt." The words rolling off her tongue sounded ridiculous in her ears and LaVet laughed.

"I will miss you," Barton said affectionately.

"What on earth will I do when you are gone?" LaVet said, forlornly, the sound of tears now strong in her tone. "How will I know myself without my compass to guide me?"

Barton stopped walking and turned to face his sister. "You are stronger than you believe, kinder than you ought to be, charitable to a fault, talented, beautiful and smarter than any women has a right to be. You are your own compass, LaVet."

"LaVet!" The sound of Frances frantically calling her name rang out in the air. Barton laughed and took up her practice sword.

"You better hurry; it sounds as if Frances is about to have an attack."

Tossing Barton the wooden sword, she gathered up her skirts and dashed toward the house. The estate home wasn't as large as a manor house but was a jewel, very picturesque and well maintained.

Frances stood in the gardens calling her name. The look of frustration on her face had become almost permanent over three years in the employ of the Roche family.

"Here, I am Frances!" she called out and waved wildly with one hand as she neared the back gardens. Frances turned to look at her and her hands flew to her hips as she glowered at LaVet.

Only three years her senior, Frances acted like a disappointed elder much of the time when dealing with LaVet. She wore her corn-colored hair pulled tightly back into a high bun; her slim wardrobe consisted only of unadorned dark dresses that where unfaltering to her figure and Frances seemed to wear a stern gaze when ever in LaVet's presence, all of this aged the maid well past her twenty-two years.

"Look at the state of you!" Frances complained as LaVet slowed to a more respectable pace and dropped her skirts. "We must hurry." Frances said and turned on her heel, leading the way toward the house.

"Are we expecting company?" LaVet pressed, falling into step behind her.

"Your father sent word ahead that he is to be arriving within the hour. He would like to meet with both you and your brother." she informed LaVet and hurried her up to her chambers.

"Father? He was not expected back for another week. I wonder what has brought him home so soon."

"We will never know if you don't get ready to greet him, and by the smell of you we will need every minute to prepare," Frances said with disapproval.

***

Frances commandeered three housemaids to assist in preparing LaVet to see her father, and by the time he had entered the house she was nearly ready. The audience with

Barton was already taking place when LaVet padded down the stairs and waited outside her father's study to welcome him home.

It wasn't long before Barton slipped out the door.

"Barton?" LaVet reached out to touch his arm as he passed. He didn't turn to face her. "Has he brought upsetting news?"

He patted her hand. "Go, he is expecting you," was all the response he offered before he left her standing outside the door.

"How was your trip, Father?" LaVet asked, placing a kiss on both cheeks as she greeted him.

"I have something to tell you." He ignored her question and indicated that she should sit down.

"What is it, Father? Is everything well? LaVet asked, concerned and taking the offered seat.

Her father laced his fingers together and took a deep breath. "Your marriage has been arranged."

"My what?"

"It will be an alliance we cannot refuse. I am anxious for this to proceed as smoothly as possible, LaVet; it will broker a much sought after peace."

As the reality of his words sank in LaVet wanted to scream and rail against her father, but held it all in as she tried to reconcile her duty with what her heart was telling her.

"Who am I to marry?" she asked, after a very long pause.

"You are going to be married to Lord Leighton in two weeks time."

"Lord Leighton? But his father…"

Cutting her off with a wave of his hand her father talked over her protest. "The feud between our families has continued for many generations but will *end* with your marriage. It was the last wish of his father and that of yours." He looked pleadingly at his youngest child and concluded, "It is a good match."

"I've seen what an arranged marriage did to Octavia, and I will not have my life end in such a way." LaVet balled both hands into fists and stood her ground.

"Do not be so dramatic. Your life will not end, nor did your sister's. You *are* my daughter and you will do as you are told." The finality in her father's voice made a cold chill run down her back.

"Please Father, I don't even know this man or anything about him… how can I marry him?"

"You are the last of three children and you are not a son. In matters like these there is little choice."

"There is always a choice, mine! I choose not to marry a man I have never met no matter how favorable a match it is. I *choose* to marry for love."

LaVet watched as her father's eyes darkened and rage swept over his features.

"I have tried to talk sense to you. You will marry Lord Leighton as arranged and I will not hear another word against it. Is that understood?" His hand came down hard on the tabletop, making LaVet jump at the sound. Rarely had she seen her father so angry and it frightened her.

Unable to find her voice, she only nodded. A few heartbeats passed and after clearing his throat he dismissed her to return to her room. LaVet fled from his presence but didn't go back to her room as her father had commanded. Instead her footsteps turned to the stables to find her solace.

The setting sun glowed red over the green hills behind the stables and the last vestiges of light poured into the stables. LaVet walked down the neatly kept rows to her horse, given to her on her nineteenth birthday. She started to rub the muzzle that met her over the top of the stable gate.

"Hello, Beauty." The large white horse nuzzled her hand, looking for a bit of sugar or apple. "I'm sorry I have nothing for you now."

"Thinking of running away?" LaVet didn't turn toward Barton as he approached.

"Yes." she answered.

"It will not solve anything." He was next to her now, a hand on her shoulder.

"I love you, Barton, but you know nothing of what I must feel. You are father's heir and will inherent Roche Manor, all his lands and wealth. You will have the chance to marry a woman of your own choosing… you could marry for love if you so wished. I… I on the other hand have been traded off like Octavia." She sighed and patted Beauty's white nose.

"Given to a man I have never met because it best suits both parties and is good for the family, I will have a loveless marriage based only on duty and honor. The most I can hope for is to not be abused or mistreated. It is the lot of a daughter."

"You make my lot in life sound so appealing. I wish it was as easy as you make it sound," Barton finally said.

"I'm sorry. I know you have much expected of you." LaVet turned to face him. "You have found me in a moment of weakness."

"No, dear LaVet, I have never seen you in weakness. Anger and passion yes, but not weakness." He placed a kiss to her forehead. "Remember who you are. Do not lose yourself and you will find happiness in your new life, I am sure."

LaVet went into her brother's embrace. "I wish mother was alive and still with us."

"She is. She is always with us."

~ Chapter Two ~

"You are going to wear out those floor boards." Kenric glanced at his grandmother and stopped his incessant pacing.

"I apologize."

"There is no need," she said and placed a hand on his arm. "I know your parents would be very proud of the choice you have made."

He stood, contemplating her comment. It was for his parents that he found himself in his current situation.

"There are moments in our lives that lead us to a crossroad. It says much about your character that you, my dear boy, are doing what is right as opposed to what is easy."

"Will there ever be a moment in life when the two are one and the same?" he asked. With a worn look he rubbed at his temple.

"Is that regret talking?" she pressed.

"No," Kenric said with finality. "This is the path my life is to take." He started to pace the floor again.

"I have… kept my thoughts on this to myself. Will you allow me now to speak openly?" Kenric looked earnestly at his grandmother as she asked the question.

"You need never feel as though you cannot speak openly with regards to me. Please do so now," he said in response.

"If you feel… even for a moment… that you might still possess any tender feelings for another… well, then this wedding should be called off immediately. It is not fair to you and certainly not to your bride-to-be."

"There is no fear in that regard. Any feelings I once held for… well they were easily disregarded once I learned of her true nature. And is it entirely fair for the two of us, myself and my intended, to enter into a marriage where is no hope of affection?"

"Then you have decided that there is no possibility of affection?" she questioned.

"Of mutual respect, of friendship; these of course can be cultivated."

"Dear boy, don't close yourself off to the possibility of more. Duty and honor have their place in this life… and so does love. Your parents were the best example of that truth." she reminded him, then watched Kenric for several moments before adding, "Go. Get some air before our guests arrive. It will do you a world of good."

"Thank you," Kenric placed a kiss to her cheek. "I will be back soon," he promised, then slipped out of the room.

The early evening air was warm and smelled of a summer breeze. Kenric had set out with no particular place in mind, but found himself on a well-known path twisting through the woods.

There was something out of place; a sound that didn't quite belong. Kenric was accustomed to the sights and sounds of this place as well as he was the walls of his childhood home. He held his horse still for a moment, both listening.

There was someone running toward him. He was sure of it, turning his horse toward the sound of approaching feet. The sound subsided and he could clearly make out the form of a woman, leaning on a nearby tree, her raven hair splayed around delicate features.

Kenric took in the distressed look on her face and disheveled dress and instantly became worried. "Pardon me miss, are you alright?" The women had clearly not seen him and jumped.

Kenric dismounted and took in her appearance more closely. "Truly you look... are you alright?" he stammered, feeling like a fool as the emerald green of her eyes took him aback as they lifted to his face.

***

LaVet looked longingly at her father and brother riding their stallions in the warm sunlight. She hated seeing Beauty tethered behind her brother's horse. Hated being laced up in a new dress and hidden from the sunlight in the dark interior of her father's carriage. Hated being tossed and jostled as they traveled. Hated each bump, each breath, and each step of the horses' hooves that took her closer to Lord Leighton and the end of everything she knew.

Her fingers closed around the letter in her lap. There wasn't sufficient light in the carriage to read the lines, but she had committed them to memory.

"My dearest LaVet,

Father has informed me of your upcoming marriage and its many advantages. You will be mistress of a great house with an honorable name. I have never met Lord Leighton myself; yet I have heard only the most positive praise connected to his name and that of his illustrious family.

As a sister I want to wish you the greatest joys in the life you now find yourself embarking on. I cannot tell you how happy I am in my own and pray for the same mutual respect between you and your husband as I have found.

I know that mother is proud of you and watches over us all. I have enclosed the necklace that she wore on the day of her marriage, the very one that was placed around my neck the day I was united with Richard. Wear it knowing that we both are there with you in heart, if not body.

With all my love, your sister,

Lady Octavia Stillwell

"My Lady, are you feeling alright?" LaVet looked up at Frances as if she had forgotten her lady's maid was seated across from her. Placing the necklace with its brilliant sapphire stone back inside the letter she held the small square of parchment as if it were a lifeline. She pressed it to her heart as the air around her became heavy, weighing down on her with great force.

"No, Frances-- I think I need some air," she said, gasping for breath and tapped the hood of the carriage hard, "Stop! Stop!" As soon as the carriage slowed LaVet pushed open the door and leapt out.

"LaVet, where are you going?" her father called as LaVet made her way to the edge of the trees lining the road.

"I need a moment, father," she said, one hand pressed to her middle, trying desperately to get air into her lungs. The letter was still clenched in the other.

"We are so near. Must we stop?" he protested.

"If we are so close a few more moments will not mater," she could hear Barton say in her defense as she slipped into the cover of the trees.

Gathering up her skirts she ran, ran as hard as the tightly laced dress would allow. It didn't matter where her flight led her or how far she went. All she knew was that she had to run, not caring that her hair was being pulled out of its bindings by branches as she rushed past.

Once the nervous energy was spent LaVet stopped running and leaned on a tree, breathing deeply of the crisp air to steady herself while the sound of her pounding heart filled her ears.

"Pardon me miss, are you alright?" LaVet jumped with surprise at no longer being alone and spun to face a tall figure seated atop a horse just a few feet from her. The sun blinded her momentarily as the stranger dismounted.

"Truly you look… are you alright?" He asked again and stepped forward, casting her into shadow. His features came into focus as her eyes adjusted. LaVet felt the breath rush from her again as her eyes met his.

His sand colored hair was tussled from a brisk run and his strongly defined features could only be described as roguishly handsome, but it was his eyes that caught and held her. She had never seen such a color before. Like the finest tempered steel, their grey was intense and piercing with a storm raging in their depths.

His gaze taking in her disheveled appearance more closely, he asked with concern, "Are you running from someone? Bandits? Have you been harmed in anyway?"

"No bandits, Sir, and I am well. Yet I have been running." He gave her a questioning look and she rushed on, "That is to say, I was running both metaphorically and truly. I have been traveling for several days and needed the fresh air. I suppose I was also running from my future, in a way."

"Is that possible?" One eyebrow rose.

"I'm afraid not. I am being married tomorrow to a man I have never met in order to ensure peace and uphold my families honor." The words rushed out before she was able to stop their escape.

"An arranged marriage then?"

"Yes," she answered.

"You seem awfully young for marriage."

"I am nineteen these eight months past. My sister was married at sixteen. By that standard I am an old maid." LaVet laughed softly at the idea.

"Well then, any offer of marriage should be accepted right away." She could hear the humor in his words and had to suppress a smile.

"Of course. I am positive that I am just the person he has always dreamed of growing old with, so there is nothing at all to fear."

"If you are truly the wife this man has always desired then why the running? It must be the groom. He is, no doubt, some kind of troll."

This time she laughed aloud. "I will soon find out. I will meet my groom this day."

"Well then, I must see you back safely to your carriage without delay." He bowed low and stepped aside to allow her to take the lead.

LaVet knew that she should feel it odd and inappropriate to be walking with a stranger, especially a man to whom she had not been properly introduced to, yet she only felt at ease. As they came near the tree line the tall stranger stopped and LaVet turned to look back at him.

"I would not want to besmirch your honor so I will say my farewells here." Then he swung easily back onto his horse. LaVet only nodded and watched as he rode away.

As she came around the last of the trees that blocked her from view Frances ran up to her in a frenzy. "My Lady! You gave us a fright! Just look at the state of you." She fussed over LaVet's dress and hair.

"Are you done acting like a child?" her father asked as he stepped up next to her; Barton holding both horses by the reins.

With a stiff lip LaVet met his gaze, "Yes, father." Then without another word she climbed back into the carriage, slipping the now crumpled letter into her handbag.

***

Kenric reined in his horse and turned it so that he was facing the road again. The raven-haired beauty he had stumbled across had safely met up with a very stern looking woman, who by the looks of it was scolding her.

Soon she was ushered into the waiting carriage and Kenric knew it was time to head back to the manor. Thinking back over their brief encounter he was sure in that moment he had just met the woman who would become his wife. The idea didn't stir in him quite the feelings he thought it ought to.

Of course neither had their conversation. Kenric smiled to himself at how easy it had been to converse with her. He had been pleasantly surprised by her candor and wit. The only thing that had left him uneasy was his own feelings. She had stirred something in him... something which had long since lay dormant.

Shaking off these fancies, he reminded himself that they knew nothing of each other beside the facts that both had been struggling with the idea of marriage and had entertained the thought of abandoning their duty. In fact, they had still to be properly introduced.

"Let's go, boy!" Kenric nudged his horse into a run in order to arrive at the manor before the carriage.

***

LaVet didn't look out at the small farms they passed or the village that stood as a gateway to Leighton Manor and her new life. She kept her eyes cast down, as with her heart, and as the carriage rolled to a stop she closed both. Becoming resolved to her fate LaVet allowed herself to be helped out of the carriage and took her first look around. The estate was larger than she had imagined; the large stone edifice of the manor house large and imposing as any castle.

Lining the great hall stood a host of maids, footmen, and other assorted staff. At the far end stood an older man, bent with age. LaVet clenched her jaw and with her father's arm approached him, all eyes on her.

"My Lord Roche, Sir Barton Roche, and Lady Roche, it is my pleasure to welcome you to Leighton Manor. I am Hugh Collingwood, head of the household." The butler bowed as low as his age would allow.

"It is very nice to meet you, Mr. Collingwood." LaVet said with genuine relief that this man was not to be her husband.

He turned and led the small group to a spacious room where a very well dressed white haired woman seated in a comfortable chair smiled broadly at them. Standing next to the chair was a tall man, dressed for riding and with the most piercing grey eyes.

LaVet stumbled as his eyes caught hers, and surprise over took any other emotion she could have been feeling at that moment. Collingwood stood at attention to make the introductions.

"Allow me to present Lord Lyman Roche, Sir Barton Roche and Lady LaVet Roche." Collingwood bowed and stepped out of the circle. "Lady Maren and Lord Kenric Leighton."

"You are all very welcome," Lady Maren said warmly, and leaning on the arm of the man LaVet now knew as Lord Leighton, she stood and offered out her hand for LaVet's father to take. "I can not tell you how much this marriage would have meant to my dearly departed husband, and now to our son, who have both often expressed a wish to bridge the gap between our families."

"It is our honor, my Lady." He lifted her hand and placed a kiss on it. Lady Maren turned to Barton and made a few kind exchanges then let her gaze fall on LaVet.

"My dear," Lady Maren took both of LaVet's hands in hers, "I do hope that you and I will become great friends. Despite our clear difference of age," she added with a smile.

"I am sure we will," LaVet assured her.

"Come here Kenric, and meet your intended." Lady Maren called to him. Her familiar way of talking to him made LaVet instantly like her. She was old enough to be brazen without it seeming rude. Kenric stepped forward and exchanged pleasantries with her father and brother, warmly welcoming them to his home.

Then his eyes turned to her. "Lady Roche." Taking her hand he bowed low and placed a brief kiss on it before releasing her. The heat of his touch remained long after his hand was withdrawn.

Kenric led his grandmother back to her chair and invited LaVet and her family to also take their rest. The men took up their conversation as LaVet sat quietly watching the exchange. Barton and Kenric both laughed heartily about something, LaVet didn't realize that she wasn't following the topic until the sound of deep full laughter rang out again. Her father shared a chuckle and even Lady Maren allowed herself a smile.

Turning her attention to them she watched the man who would become her husband closely. His manners were impeccable, his opinion agreeable, and she had to admit that his handsomeness had not diminished in the knowledge of who he was. Yet her embarrassment over the confessions of their first meeting could not be denied.

He had come upon her in a moment of vulnerability and she had done as she always had and spoke her mind without reserve. How oft had LaVet been chastised for this flaw in her person, she now regretted.

Kenric was agreeing with something her father had said, and while she gazed on she wondered what on earth he must now think of her-- this wild girl running through the woods? The idea was shocking to LaVet; that she should care *what* he thought. She had never been overly concerned for what others ever thought of her before. As Lord Roche's daughter there had always been much expected of her but LaVet had never felt as though she satisfied those expectations in the slightest.

The perfect daughter and lady had always been her sister; Barton the perfect son, and she... well, she was her father's bane, 'twas certain. Still sparring with her brother and riding a horse astride like a man, she rarely received a glance from him that wasn't disapproving.

"Dear Kenric, dinner will be served within the hour and our guests had a terribly long way to travel. I am sure that Lady Roche would like the chance to rest and refresh herself."

"Yes, you are right grandmother, I am very remiss in my proper attentions." Kenric stood then walked to LaVet and offered her his arm. "Allow me to show you to your chambers."

She laid her hand on his arm and, feeling all other eyes upon them, allowed Kenric to lead her from the room as her father and brother followed. Her eyes wandered about the manor halls as he escorted her toward the chambers they would use during their stay, all the while telling the company what lay behind closed doors or down empty corridors.

LaVet knew she would easily find herself lost in this home. It was considerably larger than her father's and very finely furnished. Taking stock of her own appearance and dress LaVet felt very out of place.

"Sir Barton, we have set up this room for your use." Kenric indicated one of the first rooms they came to. The door lay open and her brother's trunk was sitting at the end of the large bed, a warm fire already burning in the hearth.

"Lord Leighton, you are not thinking of putting us up in the family chambers?" her father protested.

"Nonsense-- after all these rooms lay empty with so little family to occupy them. They are larger and more pleasantly furnished than the guest chambers and after all, Lord Roche, are we not now family?"

Barton took his leave and her father was shown to his room as well. Suddenly LaVet was alone with Kenric, her arm still on his as he led her further down the corridor. She longed to ask him why he had kept his identity to himself during their brief encounter in the woods, but kept her silence when she realized he could ask the same of her.

"May I escort you down to dinner? Once you have been able to rest per my grandmother's request, of course," Kenric asked as he looked at her from the corner of his eye.

"I do not feel as though I require rest," she said honestly. "You have exquisite grounds here and the most beautiful home I have ever seen. I would not mind seeing more of both, if you will permit me leave to do so?"

Stopping outside an open chamber door Kenric turned to her, the full force of his gaze falling on her. "I would enjoy giving you a tour of both, yet this moment may not be the best to give way to such enjoyment." He indicated his boots, traces of mud clinging to them.

"I see. I suppose we both must make ourselves ready," she said and slipped her arm from his, daring to ask, "And did you enjoy your ride?"

"It was very… educational," he responded, then taking her hand and bowing slightly over it and then excused himself.

As LaVet watched him retreat down the corridor her hands slipped into the small handbag she held and fingered her sisters' letter. Then turning into her chambers she pulled it out. Instantly she felt something was wrong-- the letter no longer held the same weight in her palm as it had before.

Rushing to pull it open, her fear was realized when no necklace appeared there to greet her gaze. "No!" she gasped and turned the handbag inside out, spilling its contents onto the floor. Still the necklace did not reveal itself.

She turned sharply on her heel as the impulse took over to rush down to the carriage and plunder the cushions in order to retrieve the heirloom.

"Miss, what is the matter?" Frances asked as LaVet rushed right into her.

"Octavia sent me my mother's necklace and I have lost it!" she cried in despair. "It must be in my father's carriage or... or... oh, dear heavens tell me I did not drop it in the woods during my flight!"

"Stay and calm yourself; I will make sure it is searched for," Frances said in kind tones, turning LaVet back into the room. Her distress over the loss of the necklace blinded her to its fine furnishings and added comforts.

"Seat yourself, my lady. I will see to it right now." Frances waved one of the housemaids over who had been unpacking LaVet's gowns. "Please, will you see to my lady's hair and assist her out of her traveling clothes? I must see to a very important task," she explained and rushed away.

***

"I must apologize for the tardiness of your host, Lord Roche. Something very urgent and unexpected came up and Kenric was obliged to rush off with promises of returning shortly," Lady Maren said as they sat down for dinner.

"I'm sure whatever business removes him must be of great importance," her father said with a warm smile.

"You look very lovely," Lady Maren observed as she took in LaVet's appearance. The new gown fit her in style and color to accentuate each of her more attractive physical attributes. A trick she was sure her father had devised in hopes of masking those defects in her person that so often overtook any level of attractiveness she possessed.

"As do you, my lady." LaVet responded with a smile.

Lady Maren waved the compliment off and laughed, "There is no comparison 'tween a newly blooming rose and an autumn leaf."

"Can not the leaf be just as admired as a rose? Its rich color? The texture in the veins, the perfectly formed curves of its edges, the blessing of its shade, the music it makes when tossed in a summer breeze? Is not the leaf just as much a perfect creation as the rose?"

One eyebrow lifted as Lady Maren looked closely at LaVet.

"I must make apologies for my daughter," her father started, but Lady Maren cut him off with a dismissive wave.

"No, she has a right to her own mind. I welcome a woman who will speak it at such a tender age." Then turning back to LaVet she added, "You must always be completely open with me, my dear."

"You can count on it. I'm not sure my sister knows any other way but to be completely open," Barton laughed.

"In any case, I thank you for the compliment, even if I do not share the sentiment," Lady Maren nodded with kindness in her eyes at LaVet.

The conversation flowed easily as the first course was served. Barton was charming and guided each turn to a comfortable topic, complimenting Lady Maren on the manor and admiring details his keen eyes had noticed. LaVet was grateful for his easy manner and friendly disposition, both of which had placed her at ease.

Chairs scraped as Barton and her father rose when Lord Leighton entered the room. "Please sit, I apologize for my rudeness in being late to supper. I had business that could not wait to be attended to." He went right to Lady Maren.

"Grandmother," he said and placed a kiss to her cheek. She reached up and patted his face in return.

"I am glad you are back and dressed for dinner." She smiled as he took his seat at the head of the table. "I hope whatever took you away was resolved to your satisfaction?"

"Yes, it was." he answered and stole a glance at LaVet who then realized she was staring unawares. She looked away instantly and fixedly examined the second course to their dinner.

The table grew uncomfortably quiet for a few breaths before Barton came to the rescue and started up a lively conversation again. He engaged Lord Leighton in a discussion of land management that took up quite a bit of the time as the courses were served.

"Shall we retire to a more interesting pursuit while the menfolk continue to bore each other?" Lady Maren asked LaVet as she rose from the table. Kenric rushed to her side to aid her and placed her cane firmly in her grasp.

"Yes," LaVet assented, and with Barton assisting her out of her own chair came around to take Lady Maren's arm. The older lady slid her arm into LaVet's, leaning on her as Kenric relinquished his hold. There was something in his gaze she could not comprehend as it fell on her. Appreciation perhaps? For what, LaVet was uncertain.

Lady Maren led LaVet into a large brightly lit drawing room and sought respite on a low sofa.

Taking the liberty of procuring a footstool LaVet placed it near her, "Would you like to elevate your feet?" she asked.

"You are thoughtful, thank you."

"May I do anything else for your comfort?" LaVet pressed once Lady Maren's feet had been propped up on the stool.

Lady Maren seemed thoughtful for a moment; "I know this must be hard for you." she said finally.

LaVet took the chair closest by her, "It is clear that Lord Leighton loves you very much and you him. I too love my family and I understand what is being asked of me," she offered.

"Arranged marriages such as yours are not as common these days as they once were." Lady Maren closed her eyes briefly. "I am sorry, I do tire much earlier these days."

"There is no need for apologies," LaVet assured her.

"Would you do something for me?"

"If it is within my power," LaVet reassured her.

"It has been too long since this room has held the sound of music in it." LaVet looked at the pianoforte near one of the great windows.

"I would be honored to play for you," she said and walked over to the instrument.

She found a few expertly copied sheets of Steibelt's 'Grand Concerto' and studied them for a moment before placing them aside in favor of a memorized folksong with a light happy tune and silly flippant words.

When the music faded and her voice had toned its last note Lady Maren clapped politely and asked for an encore. LaVet laid out the concerto in front of her and with some hesitation worked her way through it, with each page gaining confidence as the notes resonated within her.

There was more clapping as the concerto ended and in surprise LaVet realized that they had been joined by Lord Leighton, her father and brother.

"You play beautifully," Kenric said as he approached her at the piano.

"I was not as faithful in my studies as I should have been to be a great player; nevertheless I do enjoy music."

"She is being humble," her father protested, "She plays the pianoforte with skill, yes, and she also plays the harp, the flute, and is more than proficient with the violin."

"You must show her the music room then Kenric. She will find a much better instrument than this pianoforte there and could truly play for us."

"You have a music room?" LaVet asked, looking up at Kenric from her place behind the ivory keys. She was stunning, he thought, as her large green eyes captured him in their gaze.

"Yes, it holds several of the instruments your father mentioned and a few others. It is sadly unused at the moment. Since you enjoy music, perhaps you would breathe new life into its walls?" he asked, and leaning one arm on the pianoforte he looked at her intently, enjoying the rush of color that touched her cheeks.

"Would you like to see it?" Kenric asked when LaVet made no effort to continue the conversation.

"Yes, do take her to look at it. We shall stay here, have a rousing game of cards where these gentlemen will allow me to win and then we shall all retire. After all, tomorrow is a very big day for us all." his grandmother said and patted the open seat close to her indicating that Barton should take it.

"Shall we?" Kenric asked and held out his hand for LaVet, who took it, stood and allowed him to guide her from the room. Taking up one small candle with him as he did so, Kenric led her along in silence. She kept stealing glances at him, wondering about this man. Soon his steps slowed and then stopped.

"Wait here while I light the room," He instructed and slid his arm from hers. Pushing open the heavy doors he disappeared inside, then slowly the grand room glowed into focus.

The room was large with vaulted ceilings, yet was pleasantly decorated and held a warm and inviting air. The far wall glittered in the candle light as tall cathedral stain glassed windows reflected the glow. Kenric momentarily realized that chamber, with all its grandeur, still paled in comparison to the woman pausing just inside its doors.

He watched LaVet venture in, her graceful movements as fluid and graceful as a dancer. She drifted to the center of the room and allowed her fingers to brush over the tall golden gilded pedal harp. "I've never seen such a collection of harps," she breathed as her fingers brushed over the bronze wires.

"Do you play the pedal harp?" Kenric asked from the opposite side of the large room, where he had a perfect vantage point to watch her.

"I have had very few chances to play on one. I am more familiar with Irish wire-strung lap harp, the folk harp, and double-strung folk and Welsh triple harps."

"Your brother did not exaggerate your musical abilities then?" he laughed.

"My mother was very passionate about music and stressed that part of my education. I can play every instrument held in this room to one level or another, yet none half as well as I should."

"I've had the pleasure of hearing you play one instrument already and I didn't find it lacking." Kenric was shocked by his own boldness with the statement.

"There is no need to flatter me, Lord Leighton." LaVet said and turned her attention to a second instrument. The comment took Kenric back a pause. He had never been, nor ever would have, considered himself a flatterer for flattery's sake. Honesty in all his dealings was uppermost in his mind. For her to assume that he did not mean the compliment surprised him.

"Lady Roche, you have no reason to believe me at the moment, but I do not give compliments lightly. I have no high regard for flippancy. I was honest in my praise of your ability, or what I have had the pleasure of witnessing thus far." She looked back at him now, her full lips held slightly apart as she studied him as if to gauge his sincerity.

Kenric reasoned that she must have made up her mind when, taking a deep breath, she stepped forward and asked, "Was this room for your mother's use?" For an instant Kenric stiffened at the mention of his mother, then the moment was gone and his easy air returned.

"When the manor was being constructed this was meant to be the family's private chapel and was built to have impeccable acoustics, but near completion great-great grandfather decided it would be better for the family to attend services in the village, to maintain a relationship with those who live on our land.

"So, consequently, this room became the family's music room. The collection of instruments and music have been compiled over four generations. I'm sad to say that since the passing of my parents it has not been in use as it should be."

His eyes followed her as LaVet moved over to a masterfully handcrafted violin. "This is exquisite," she whispered.

Kenric cleared his throat. "I'm glad you like it."

"I have yet to see anything in your home that isn't pleasing." It seemed as though LaVet would continue, but she hesitated.

As her eyes rested on him again Kenric detected a flicker of sadness that made him frown. "I know this... situation we both find ourselves in isn't ideal."

With a quick devilish smile LaVet responded, "Am I to understand that I am *not*, in fact, just the person you have always dreamed of growing old with?" She was clearly teasing him by referring to their conversation in the woods.

The glimpse of the woman he had met sent a smile across his features. "Well, that depends, have you decided yet?"

"Decided on what?" she asked, confused.

"Am I the troll you expected?"

LaVet coughed back a laugh at his question. "I believe the troll was your analogy, not mine. You knew then-- when we met in the woods-- that I was your betrothed, didn't you?"

"I did work that bit out, yes," he confirmed as the corners of his lips twisted upward.

"Why didn't you tell me who you were?" she asked, taking a step in his direction.

"For a short moment I wasn't Lord Kenric Leighton and you were not my betrothed. And in that moment you were completely honest."

"You were afraid I would be dishonest with you, my Lord?"

"No, not dishonest," he protested, "But not wholly forthcoming. The instant your eyes fell upon me during our formal introduction I feared that your openness would be tempered by the knowledge of who I was and the nature of our forthcoming relationship."

"It is not in my nature to play games. I do tend to tease, but I am honest to a fault and find it physically impossible to bide my tongue. If you have not been already warned of this shortcoming I'm sure my father will be quick to remedy his oversight," she assured him with her eyes downcast.

Kenric took a slow pace toward her. "I am glad to hear it. I would not wish for anything but total and open honesty between us."

"I must admit, my Lord, I do find myself at a loss. I have no earthly idea how to conduct myself. I am continuously in raptures over almost everything I see around me and I feel horribly out of place amongst such finery. I am afraid you will profoundly regret your decision to enter into this arrangement with someone as unrefined and uncultured as I."

Once again Kenric moved to bridge the gap between them by taking a step forward while LaVet spoke.

"I know something of how you must have felt when this arrangement was presented to you." Kenric's voice was low as he addressed her. He had noticed that her emotions were clearly displayed in her expressions and he watched her closely now as he spoke. "I… I can't promise you love, yet you will never want for anything, you will never be mistreated or abused, and I hope you will come to be happy here at Leighton Manor."

***

LaVet wasn't able to shake the feeling that Kenric hadn't said everything he wished to. It took her several moments to answer as she processed the scope of her future life as he had described it.

"I thank you for your kind words and assurances on my behalf. In truth, I have little idea of what I was expecting upon arriving. It may take me some time to be fully myself or at ease with these new surroundings and responsibilities," she said finally, adding in a much softer voice, "I will try not to be… a disappointment to you." It wasn't the sentiment LaVet wished to convey, but she wasn't sure how best to express the feelings of inadequacy she was wrestling with. Finding so much at fault in her character, stature, dress and manners to be the mistress of such a fine home was overwhelming her.

"I have yet to see anything disappointing," he said as his careful steps now brought him close enough that LaVet was forced to tilt her head back in order to look at him.

Kenric didn't wait for her to respond before he continued, "I have something I would like to give you."

He felt in the pocket of his waistcoat and pulled out a small glittering item. She gasped in utter disbelief as he deposited her mother's sapphire necklace into her open palm.

~ Chapter Three ~

On the day of her wedding LaVet awoke to Frances humming and pulling back the heavy curtains; early morning light spilling into the room.

"I've brought your breakfast," Frances said, and as LaVet sat up in bed she placed the heavily laden tray of food onto her lap.

"I do not feel at all hungry," LaVet protested and wrinkled her nose.

"Miss, you must eat. Today is your wedding."

"Thank you Frances, I am aware of what day it is," she said and pushed the tray off to one side.

"It must be nerves." Frances said with a sly smile. "I imagine that many women would feel the same in your place. He is very handsome, I dare say."

Giving Frances a look of disgust LaVet slid from bed and stood. "My hunger has little to do with how handsome Lord Leighton is or is not."

"Yes, my Lady," Frances said, trying to suppress a smile as she fussed over LaVet and untied her nightdress.

"I do have a question for you, Frances."

"What can I help you with?" Frances asked as she directed LaVet to a warm bath.

"Last night Lord Leighton handed me my mother's necklace. Do you have any idea where he found it? Or how he knew it belonged to me?"

"He did not tell you himself?" Frances asked, her brow furrowed.

"No, I didn't have the chance to ask him. My father entered the room and ended the opportunity for conversation."

"Well, last evening when I rushed out of your chambers to look in the carriage Lord Leighton stopped me in the hall, inquiring if anything was amiss. I told him about the missing necklace. Was I wrong to do so?"

"No you did nothing wrong. Yet I still don't see how it came to be in his possession?" LaVet curled forward in the tub while Frances scrubbed her hair with something that smelled of wildflowers.

"He did ask if he could escort me to the stables but when we reached them he asked a man named Gallagher-- his steward I believe-- to assist me and to saddle his horse. Before I was done with my search he was mounted and gone. I have no idea how he came to have the necklace," Frances went on. She began rinsing out LaVet's tresses.

"Could his steward have found it?"

"It is possible, my lady. Although that would beg the question as to why it wasn't presented to me earlier, upon its retrieval. Perhaps after I made my own search it was found by one of the stable hands," Frances concluded with confidence.

"Yes, that must be the answer." LaVet agreed. Then another thought crossed her mind. Frances said that Kenric left shortly after he escorted her to the stables. At dinner they had been informed some urgent business called him away and so was late to join them. Was it possible that he had ridden out to where their encounter in the woods took place to look for the heirloom? And even more incredible, had found it? The idea that he would go to such lengths was absurd and she pushed it from her mind.

"We had better get you dry before the water turns cold; I wouldn't want you to catch a chill." Frances brought LaVet out of her thoughts.

Sooner than LaVet expected she was standing in front of a long mirror looking at herself as the white dress was laced up. Her raven hair was pulled, twisted, braided and rolled into an attractive arrangement about her head and dotted with small white flowers. Her checks were patted and pinched to give them a rosy color, her lips tinted and neck dabbed with a sweet scented perfume. Once the veil was placed on her head she was almost unable to recognize herself in the reflection.

"Oh Miss LaVet, you are a vision." Frances said and clapped her hands together, surveying her work with approval.

LaVet looked from the woman in white she could no longer see as herself to Frances and reached out to take her maid's hand. "Thank you."

"Of course."

There was a light tapping at the chamber door and Frances moved to answer it. Lady Maren didn't wait to be invited or introduced and glided into the room. Her eyes took in LaVet and a wide smile spread across her face.

"Perfection," she stated.

"You are too kind, Lady Maren." LaVet protested.

"You are too young to be so modest, my dear. And I am too old to be kind," she said with a chuckle. "You look very beautiful."

Frances moved to offer Lady Maren a chair and she seemed grateful to take her ease. Once seated she looked back to LaVet, "I know I can not stand in the place of your mother or sister; however, I would like to offer you what fond counsel I can."

"It would be an honor, Lady Maren, to have you stand in their place." LaVet went to her; bending at the knee to look her in the eye she gathered Lady Maren's hands together in her own. "I am not an easy person to befriend, but I feel you and I will rub along well."

"First I must teach you the ability to accept a compliment."

LaVet laughed at her comment, then with a smile asked, "As you do, Lady Maren? If so, then I suppose we are both lost to the art of accepting flattery, are we not?" she said, reminding Lady Maren that she too had brushed off a kind observation.

Lady Maren didn't press the subject but gave LaVet a rueful smile. "I'd like to give you this to carry with you today." Reaching into her small hand bag Lady Maren retrieved a very delicate and exquisitely embroidered handkerchief.

"It's lovely, did you make it?"

"Oh heavens no, I have not this level of talent." Pressing it into LaVet's hand she sighed, "Kenric's mother made this shortly before she... before she was taken from us. I believe she would wish you to have it."

LaVet studied the handkerchief with reverence. "I will keep it always, thank you."

***

The notion that she should feel something more than duty didn't occur to her until LaVet had left her father's arm and her hand had been taken by Kenric. As their eyes met she noted a dark storm raging within their depths.

Together they took their place in the front of the chapel. LaVet felt the tightening of a knot in the pit of her stomach as she vowed to honor and respect him. Her mind spun as Kenric repeated his vows, his eyes never leaving hers. Every part of the interaction felt otherworldly until he slipped a gold band on her finger and swept her into his arms to press a kiss to her lips.

The effect the kiss had on her was astounding and her breath caught in her lungs. Then abruptly it was over, and LaVet felt dizzy as Kenric escorted her from the church amidst the cheers of their families and a few select members of the congregation.

***

Pouring a second drink Kenric swallowed the burning liquid in one swallow and set the empty glass down slightly harder than intended. A glimmer of light flashed and Kenric's eyes were drawn to his wedding band.

He let out a long, low sigh then poured another drink in an attempt to drown out the sound of his heart pounding in his ears. It was time, he told himself. Leaving the glass drained yet again he walked up the stairs leading to the family bedchambers and tapped lightly on LaVet's door.

There was a sound of rustling but no response. Again Kenric tapped.

"Shall I answer that?" he heard LaVet's lady's maid ask. There was no clear response and Kenric waited. The door opened and he was admitted as the maid excused herself and took her leave.

LaVet stood still as a statue, long locks of black hair spilling down her shoulders as she clutched her robe tightly around her. She looked very frightened as all the color drained out of her face, leaving her ashen.

Kenric noted the slight shaking of her shoulders and wished to calm her. "May we sit down and talk?" he asked and gestured to the chairs near the fire. Kenric waited until LaVet had taken her seat before he sat at the edge of his.

"I should have tried to discuss this subject last night when we spoke... yet, based on its delicate nature I wasn't comfortable discussing it until after the vows had been exchanged," Kenric barreled forward, the few drinks he had now giving him courage.

"You need not feel uneasy about discussing any subject with me," she reassured him in a small voice.

Kenric nodded, "Neither of us are under any delusion as to the nature of this marriage. With that said, I would like to reassure you that I am expecting no more from the arrangement than what is proper." He watched as LaVet visibly flinched. Unable to sit and stare at her he shot to his feet and moved to stand behind the chair, gripping the back as if it were a lifeline.

"As my wife you will be asked to see to the sick and poor in the village. To run this household and see to the needs of my grandmother, to be at my side during public appearances, show support for my decisions and to give counsel when needed. Beyond those things I will not ask." Kenric made a point to stress the last few words in order for his meaning to become clear to her and then waited with bated breath for her reply.

When LaVet didn't raise her head or make any attempt to clarify his words Kenric ground his teeth together and cursed inwardly at how uncomfortable their situation had become. He longed for the levity of yesterday.

"We will continue to keep separate bedchambers," Kenric finally added.

LaVet looked at him in the golden glow cast by the fire, then forced out a weak, "If you think that is best," and allowed her eyes to drop back to her hands.

"I've upset you," Kenric interpreted her silence and ran a hand through his hair in frustration.

"No," she replied, still unable to meet his gaze.

"I do not... that is, I am not the kind of man that would take liberties... make advances where they are not welcome."

"There is no need to explain further, my lord; I understand you perfectly," LaVet countered then closed her eyes.

"I will take my leave. Good night." LaVet made no attempt to answer his farewell.

Later, as Kenric sat in his study, his eyes locked on the fire as he relived their conversation. He was fully aware of how terribly awkward their marriage would be for some time as they grew to know each other and he expected a great many obstacles.

But she had looked so frightened... or was it repulsion that he had seen? Was LaVet unable to think of him as anything more than the means to ending their families' feud? Kenric felt anger surge through him. Of course she was repulsed-- how could she be anything else? Had he really expected her to... to what? Throw herself at his feet and beg him to stay?

She had been at Leighton Manor only two days and in that time her entire life had changed. A new home, new people, a new name and all that entailed... and soon her family would leave, only increasing her isolation from anything familiar. By comparison, little if nothing would really change drastically in Kenric's life upon the marriage.

With this revelation in mind he determined to make the transition as painless for LaVet as possible, even if that meant staying away from her.

***

"Must you go?" LaVet clung to Barton's arm as they took a turn through the gardens.

"I'm afraid so, Little Bit." She smiled at the use of her childhood nickname then sighed.

"I hate the idea of being left here alone."

Barton laughed, "My dear little sister, you are hardly alone. You will have more than your share of company and responsibilities to even notice my absence. Or that of Father's."

"Can it really only be ten days since our arrival? It feels more like years." LaVet stopped walking and turned to look at the large manor house. "Is this place really to be my home?"

"It is a beautiful and imposing place, to be sure. Yet, I have a very good feeling that you will find yourself to be happy here." Barton's gaze was also on the stone edifice in the distance; the house staff bustling in and out as her father's carriage was made ready for their departure.

"I do not share your positive view on my future, I'm afraid. How could Father ever believe I would be happy in a place where it is clear I am not wanted in the slightest?"

"Sulking does not suit you." Barton moved to stand in front of LaVet and took her by both hands. "Little Bit, there are things in this life that are out of our control. Those things do not matter. What does matter, however, is our reaction to those things.

"You have fallen captive to an arranged marriage. No matter what the packaging may look like, aren't they all but arrangements in the end? One woman marries for position and fortune, the next for comfort and security, another for love. Each is a different form of the larger picture. After the vows, each day is a new opportunity to become something greater than ones self, regardless of how the arrangement may have started."

Barton looked at her hard for a long moment before continuing, "You are free to make this your prison… or your home. It is now not Father's decision or your husband's. It is yours. I know you; you are lively and bright, full of joy and kindness. You have much to add to this place, to the lives you touch. Do not let the beginning dictate the ending. Choose something better, to *be* someone better every day, and you will find your happiness."

"When did you become so wise?" she asked with tears in her eyes as they resumed their slow walk back to the house.

"Oh dear sister, I've always been wise. It's a burden really," he said in jest and laughed when LaVet hit him hard in the waistcoat for it.

"You are right. I have been… sulking," she relented.

"And are you done?"

"I believe so. But do not judge me for shedding a tear upon your departure."

"Just one tear?" Barton pressed.

"You will have to stay away a terribly long time to deserve more than one," she smiled back.

"I hope it will not be too long a time before we are able to meet again." Their steps slowed as they reached the front of the house where their father was waiting along with Lady Maren, Kenric and Frances.

"Have you said your goodbyes?" their father asked, bending to place a kiss on LaVet's cheek.

"Not goodbye, just au revoir—'until we meet again', Father." she countered.

"Until then," he nodded in approval then turned to shake hands with Kenric and bow to Lady Maren in departure.

"Remember what I said," Barton whispered in her ear as he gave her a hug.

"I will try," she promised. "You will write, won't you?"

"Every officer needs a faithful correspondent and I expect to be kept abreast of all the news." He smiled and placed his own kiss to her cheek.

LaVet batted her eyelids rapidly to force back the welling tears and waved as her father and beloved brother drove off in the carriage, their mounts trailing behind.

Beside her Kenric offered a handkerchief for her use. "Thank you," was all she could murmur as she took it and dabbed at her eyes.

"Is there anything I can do?" he asked in a low voice.

LaVet shook her head. "No, my lord. If it is permitted, I think I will retire to my chambers."

Looking solemn, Kenric only stepped aside and allowed her to pass.

~ Chapter Four~

Dearest Octavia,

I was overjoyed to receive your last letter. These past four weeks at Leighton Manor have been exceedingly busy ones as I try to take my footing as mistress. June has come and gone and I have been blessed with the correspondence of both Barton and Father. Each seem equally well, although Father does seem to be more lonely than he may have anticipated now that all his children are away from home.

I have had the opportunity to meet with several of the individuals who live in the village of Tredan (a township on Leighton property), and was introduced to those attending church services. I'm very impressed with our clergyman and his kind wife. We have been twice to visit the sick and widowed together and she is a great help to me.

You asked in your last letter how I felt about running such a large household, and I must confess that I have found it much more challenging than I had anticipated. Lady Maren is very kind in helping to direct me in the right path when I feel less than capable. I have asked her to continue in creating the daily menus. I am hopeless when it comes to those things, as you well know.

As to your second query, I have not yet had the chance to go hunting, shooting or any of the unladylike activities you listed, although I do not think any of them would shock or surprise my husband as you suggest. Nor would he be interested in knowing the many ways in which I will disappoint him in the future. I believe any kind of marriage should have its share of surprises; why deprive him of his so soon?

In any case, Lord Leighton has been gone a fortnight and so has not had the chance to observe me and my shortcomings. He is expected to return soon with friends. I look forward to having others to converse with, for we have not met with any new

company these long weeks. I have been informed that our closest neighbor of any rank is

in Bath to take the waters. I suppose Lady Abney and I are expected to be great friends

when she does return. I will keep you apprised.

Pray tell me news of your family-- how are the children? And of you dear

Octavia, I would beg also to hear.

With affection, your sister,

LaVet Leighton

As she ended her correspondence and addressed it for delivery the sound of

hooves on gravel took her attention, and laying the letter aside LaVet stood and went to

the window. Below two horsemen were riding up to the manor. She could tell in an

instant that one of them was indeed her husband.

Gathering up her letter LaVet rushed to find Collingwood. "Would you please

have this sent out with the two penny post?" she asked, handing it to him.

"Yes, my lady."

"Thank you, Collingwood." LaVet left the butler and hurried into the large sitting

room where Lady Maren was seated, needlework in hand.

"My dear, are you done with your letter already?" she asked upon seeing LaVet.

"I am." LaVet sat across from her and wished she too had something useful to

occupy her hands.

"My eyes are not what they once were. I fear this will have to be undone and re-

stitched." Lady Maren sighed and lowered her needlework to her lap in defeat.

"You are every bit the perfectionist Lady Maren. Your skill surpasses anyone I have ever known and still you find fault with it," LaVet observed.

"If I am a perfectionist it is because I have had the time to become so. Skill has little to do with it," she protested.

"Pardon me, Lady Leighton, Lady Maren," Collingwood said from the door as he bowed low to each of them, "Lord Leighton and Sir Alistair Fitzroy have just arrived. They will be in directly to join you."

Collingwood bowed out and as he shut the door Lady Maren grumbled, "Alistair Fitzroy the parasite."

"Who is Alistair Fitzroy?" LaVet pressed, intrigued by Lady Maren's reaction to his name.

"He is an old friend of Kenric's. As boys they were both as good as any you can imagine. I'm sad to say that not all men grow to be as honorable as Kenric. Alistair inherited a title from his father, then with the help of his twit of a wife squandered everything else away. Accustomed to a genteel living since birth, but unable to support such a life style, they are now next to destitute.

"With pecuniary stresses at home Fitzroy now travels and lives off the charity of wealthy friends, leaving his wife and children for months at a time. It is a poor way of dealing with one's problems. And if that were not enough to earn my displeasure, then his constant schemes and speculations that he endeavors to drag Kenric into would do it. The man is determined to ruin everyone."

"If it is as you say, then why would Lord Leighton keep his company?"

"Kenric is blinded by the friend he once knew and feels as though he can help him, I suppose." The sound of men's voices reached them from outside the door and Lady Maren gave LaVet a look of foreboding and said quietly, "Prepare yourself."

The door opened and Kenric appeared. LaVet knew the warning had been for the short, slightly rounder and fair-haired man that followed him, but it was the sight of her husband that struck her.

"Kenric." Lady Maren beamed as he walked to her and placed a kiss on her cheek.

"Hello Grandmother."

His grey eyes turned on LaVet. Lifting her eyes to look at him she tried to smile around the bundle of nerves she had become with his appearance. He stepped to her and she allowed Kenric to raise her up, both her hands in his.

"Hello," He said and leaned in to place a kiss on her cheek. LaVet felt awkward as she returned the greeting.

"It is good to have you home," she whispered as he straightened.

"This can't be she!" The man she assumed was Alistair Fitzroy laughed in a booming voice and stepped closer. "This vision cannot be *your* wife? I refuse to believe that anyone as beautiful as this angel would consent to marry you."

Kenric stepped to one side of LaVet, allowing his friend a full view of her and letting her hands slip from his grasp.

"LaVet, I would like to introduce my friend Sir Alistair Fitzroy. Fitzroy, this is indeed my wife. The Lady LaVet Leighton."

Fitzroy rushed forward and took up one of LaVet's hands, kissing the back of it a little longer than appropriate. He smelled strongly of drink and LaVet had to stop herself from wrinkling her nose at the stench.

"I am honored to meet you, Sir Fitzroy," she said politely.

"It is my honor, truly." He smiled. The action was meant to be inviting and warm but only left LaVet feeling as though she needed to wash. It was abundantly clear that Sir Fitzroy had not only been drinking but was well beyond his limit as he was slightly unsteady on his feet.

She pulled her hand away, "You must be tired after your travels. Would you care to take a respite before dinner?"

"I would never wish to be far away from such magnificent company, but I should dress for the occasion." He bowed to her and then seemed to notice he had forgotten to greet Lady Maren.

"My Lady, you are more--"

"Do not waste your flattery on me, Fitzroy," she stopped him short, "I do not need it, nor welcome it." Lady Maren stood, reaching for the bell-pull.

"Collingwood will see me to my chambers so I can dress for dinner." She waved Kenric back when he made to step to her side and with cane in hand made her way to the door.

"It is some time until dinner," Kenric said with concern as Collingwood appeared in the door.

"If I am to endure more of his nonsense and flowery words mixed with gratuitous amounts of liquor, I will need sometime to lay down and mentally prepare." She pointed her cane in Fitzroy's direction who just laughed off the barb and made himself very much at home in the nearest chair.

"It is good to be among friends once more," was Fitzroy's only reply.

***

Over breakfast the next morning Fitzroy informed LaVet and Lady Maren that he had asked Kenric to accompany him on a business trip.

"Is it really necessary for him to attend to this business? He is a newly married man and may enjoy some more time at home," Lady Maren pointed out as she placed her teacup in its saucer.

"Kenric is a very lucky man indeed," Fitzroy gave LaVet a brief nod. "He did show a high interest when I made the offer for him to attend me. I am looking into a new venture and require his opinion."

"And this investment needs his immediate consideration?" LaVet questioned.

"I doubt it is his consideration that is so desperately needed, so much as his pocketbook." Lady Maren commented.

"Lady Maren, the nature of commerce is better left to those who comprehend such, don't you believe?" Fitzroy gave her a look that said he felt women should be seen and not heard as his tone dripped with condescension.

LaVet bristled at the implication. "Excuse me, Sir Fitzroy, it is my belief that all those who could be affected should have a clear knowledge of any dealings that could have a bearing on their future. Whatever this venture or speculation is, as a superior member of this household Lady Maren is well within her rights to question it."

"And your father discussed all major decisions with *you* before they were made, I take it." Fitzroy feigned interest.

"I was not his elder, nor his wife," LaVet pointed out then added, "My mother was involved not only in the running of the household, but my father sought her counsel on those things that affected us all."

"Each man is entitled to run his home the way he sees fit, I suppose," he said flippantly, dismissing both women.

LaVet had instantly disliked Fitzroy upon their introduction, but the more the man talked the more she found herself wondering why he and Kenric were friends. She had thought her husband had more sense than to be taken in by such a man as Fitzroy.

"Good morning," Kenric said to the room at large as he entered. "Fitzroy and I are going for a ride today; would you like to join us?"

LaVet was momentarily taken aback by the question, having spent so little time with Kenric in the past month.

"I would indeed."

"I'm glad; I've already asked to have Beauty saddled for you." He smiled at her as he took his seat at the head of the table. "I'm sorry I was late, there was some estate business I had to attend to."

"Was this estate business something you needed a second opinion on? Could one of us perhaps be of help?" Fitzroy asked and then took a long sip of his tea.

"Thank you Fitz, but it was easily remedied." LaVet noticed the look of satisfaction that crossed Fitzroy's face at Kenric's comment and realized Fitzroy was clearly telling her that she was not important enough to be consulted-- to know her place.

***

Kenric took his riding hat and gloves from Collingwood and thanked him. Standing outside with Fitzroy as they waited for LaVet to make herself ready to join them, he squinted toward the house in an attempt to catch a glimpse of her.

"Damn waste of time if you ask me. You didn't need to extend the invitation to *her*. We could be off already, not to mention that we will not be able to keep a good clip while waiting all day for a lady rider." Fitzroy hit the tip of his riding crop on his boot.

"Fitz, you are my oldest friend," Kenric turned to him. "And being thus I feel as though I can say openly that no matter the amount of drink you have consumed on any given day, you will not be allowed to insult my wife again. Is that quite understood?"

"Kenric, my good man! She is only a woman. They are all alike and none of them trustworthy. You are newly married, but trust me old friend, you will see in time that I am right. It is better to distance yourself from her now and avoid any heartache. Find yourself a pretty mistress and make the most of your life while you can." Fitzroy pulled a flask from his waistcoat and took a long drink.

Kenric felt an almost overwhelming need to punch Fitzroy in the mouth. With every word uttered he felt more and more protective of LaVet. Knowing Fitzroy as well as he did, Kenric was able to discern from whence his words sprang, and thus gave Kenric pause.

"I'm sorry to have kept you waiting." LaVet's voice brought Kenric out of the darker recesses of his mind and he turned from Fitzroy.

At the sight of her he instantly relived the moment he had laid eyes on her after returning home, instantaneously comprehending that he had made a great misstep by keeping away so long. In his absence Kenric had attempted to push her from his thoughts but it had been useless.

This was reaffirmed when he had taken her hands in his and greeting. There was little help for it; Kenric was in trouble. His heart was in very real jeopardy, and LaVet was left blissfully unaware of the war now raging within him.

"Shall we?" she asked with a smile when neither man acknowledged her arrival.

"Yes," Kenric muttered, and remembering himself moved to assist LaVet in mounting Beauty. "Would you like the mounting block?" he asked, then watched in astonishment as she stepped nimbly into one stirrup and swung her other leg up, landing in the saddle securely astride.

What he had assumed was a long riding habit with fashionable buttons running down both sides of the skirt was in fact a full set of riding breeches that gave her the look of propriety with the freedom to ride in whatever manner she chose. He had never seen such a riding habit before.

LaVet caught his look, "If you prefer, I could have her re-saddled and ride sidesaddle; it is still in the tack room-- is it not, Collingwood?" she asked the older manservant who had not yet returned to the house.

"Perfect, another delay," Fitzroy muttered.

Ignoring him, Kenric shook his head. "No, if you prefer to ride astride I will not say anything against it." He was still mildly astonished as he mounted his own horse and gripped the reins.

It wasn't unheard of for some women to ride astride but it was not something seen often in genteel society, and Kenric wondered if he should insist that she ride sidesaddle.

This idea soon left his head when on her command the white horse bolted forward in almost a dead run toward the high fields.

"By George, she can ride!" Kenric agreed with Collingwood, who was standing a few feet away, his hand shading his eyes as he watched LaVet race across the grounds.

"I guess that's our cue to get moving." Fitzroy prodded his mount to follow and Kenric clicked his tongue.

After a time the three met up and the ride slowed to a mild clip where conversation became possible.

"I have never in my life seen anything like you astride that horse," Kenric mused.

"Yes, it is quite the vulgar display," Fitzroy muttered.

LaVet acted as though she had not heard him, "My mother insisted that I play all manner of musical instruments, but my true passion lay in a very different direction. I have been riding for longer than my memory stretches... or so my brother will attest."

"And you prefer to shun convention and ride as if you were a man," Fitzroy scoffed and forced his horse to outflank them, riding ahead.

"Have I done something to displease your friend?" she asked when Fitzroy had moved beyond hearing.

"No, he is... difficult at the best of times. Although it was not always the truth he has become a hard man these last years and has little complimentary to say about women. Please, do not take it personally."

"I will try," she said, and he watched as she leaned forward to pat the large white horse on the neck. "You have me at a disadvantage Lord Leighton?" LaVet said, glancing at him from the corner of her eye.

"How so?" he asked with interest.

"The few times we have conversed you have shown interest in my pursuits and interests but reveal little of yourself. I feel as though I know nothing about you."

Kenric thought over each time he had found himself in conversation with her and concluded she was right. "Unfortunately, I am a very dull man and I do believe you could sketch my person with merely a few queries."

"I dare say that I believe I would find you rather interesting," LaVet commented, and instantly looked away from him as the color in her cheeks deepened. Kenric was enthralled with how the touch of pink highlighted her already delicate features.

"I meant that… from what I have been able to already glean, you and I share similar interests." This comment caught his interest.

"Tell me what you have learned already and I'll supply the rest," he encouraged.

He noted that she kept her eyes focused in front of them rather than on him as she answered, "I know you enjoy music, or at least that is the impression I've received."

"I do. I spent many hours in the music room as a youth, listening to my mother play. What else?"

"You enjoy the outdoors."

"How did you come to that conclusion?"

"Why would any man keep two very fine thoroughbreds of Arabian descent if not for hunting? Or do you prefer to race them? Either way, both are outdoor activities. You also keep four carriage horses and I did take note of the small Welsh Cob."

"You know your horses," Kenric commented in surprise.

"Barton is the true authority. I've taken a few things here and there."

"You have guessed correctly; I do enjoy the outdoors and good weather."

"I would also venture that you are well-read and like to be informed on a wide range of topics. I observed that the collection of books in your study is almost as large as that might be found in a true library-- although not as neatly shelved." Kenric was pleased when she exchanged a slight smile with him.

"What in the blazes are the two of you going on about? Kenric, I thought we were to ride today... not stand still and chat." Fitzroy snapped as he reined his horse in closely to Kenric and LaVet, who were ambling along at a slow pace.

"I do apologize, Sir Fitzroy. I have detained Lord Leighton long enough. Please do not stand upon ceremony on my account." There was a marked coolness in her address. "Thank you for inviting me to join you but I am growing tired." Without waiting for a reply she turned her horse in the direction of the house and was gone.

***

Beauty nickered and bounced her nose under LaVet's hand. "Sorry girl, I suppose I'm distracted today." She patted the velvety nose then started to work on rubbing down Beauty's neck.

"We had a good run today, didn't we girl?" LaVet talked to the snow-white face and large brown eyes that blinked back at her.

"She is an amazing animal." LaVet tried to hide her surprise at Kenric's sudden appearance.

"She is," LaVet agreed.

"I'm sorry these last few days have been quite hectic with Fitz here. We haven't been able to talk since our last ride together," Kenric said, opening his palm to offer

Beauty a sugar lump. It had been just over seven days since Kenric's return and in that time Fitzroy had made great demands on his time.

"Are you really leaving this afternoon for London?" LaVet asked.

"I won't be gone long; these...trips with Fitz never are extended."

"I wish you weren't going," LaVet said honestly. Lifting her eyes she noticed the raised eyebrows and curious look Kenric gave her.

"Is there a *particular* reason you wish me to stay?" he asked, his voice low.

"Forgive me for saying so, but I do not trust Sir Alistair Fitzroy. I do not believe that he has your best interests at heart."

Kenric's features darkened. "I see Grandmother has been bending your ear."

"She is entitled to her opinion of him, as am I. Mine was formed on my own, and I am insulted at the implication that I am not capable of knowing my own mind."

"Forgive me," Kenric straightened. "I did not come here to have an augment."

"He is your friend, and thus I have been gracious and I have borne his excessive drinking and rudeness. I have not once expressed my displeasure with his barbs and insults in regards to the weaker sex. Frankly, I have never heard a man speak so much ill of his own wife or so little of his children.

"In my mind it indicates to a greater flaw in his character that deeply troubles me, particularly if his power and influence over you is become injudicious. So yes, I do not wish you to go. I do not trust him and... and I would worry." LaVet bit back any further remarks on Fitzroy, seeing the storm in Kenric's eyes darken with her every word.

Kenric studied her for several moments, "Has he truly made you so uncomfortable?" He finally pressed.

"I am sorry… I… I am not used to tempering my words. If you feel that you must go, I will of course support that decision." The words felt heavy on her tongue as she said them.

Kenric let out a long breath. "If you will allow me, I'd like to change the subject."

"Of course." Stepping out from behind Beauty she addressed him. "What would you like to discuss?" Absentmindedly she reached up and grasped the necklace hanging around her neck and rubbed it between two fingers.

"Grandmother presented the idea to me of having a ball in your honor. Such an event would introduce the new Lady Leighton to our friends and acquaintances."

"A ball?" she said in surprise, as together they walked out of the stables and into the warmth of the day.

"Are you opposed to the idea?" he inquired.

From the corner of her eye she glanced up at him. "Not entirely, my Lord."

"You do not care to dance? We could hold a day of sport or a picnic." he suggested.

LaVet smiled, "I do dance and enjoy it very much… yet, I am not a peacock. I have never craved nor wanted to be the center of attention and the idea of it makes me feel very… nervous." Her hand fell away from the necklace and she folded her arms across her middle.

"A peacock?" One corner of his mouth twitched.

"A lady that primps and struts for the pure enjoyment of onlookers."

A laugh, deep and rich, burst from Kenric. "I have never heard it described such but yes, I would have to agree, *you* are not a peacock." He continued to laugh and LaVet found the sound of it pleasant and realized that she had only heard its tone once before. The sound was illuminating, like the clouds opening to allow streams of sunlight pour down.

"It's a beautiful gem," he commented while smiling over at her. LaVet didn't realize she had reached up to touch the necklace again.

"It was my mother's. I... I never did thank you properly for returning it to me. Thank you." She exchanged a meaningful look with him as they reached the house, where Lady Maren was taking in the sun and a cup of tea on the back terrace. She waved the two of them over eagerly.

"Has my grandson asked you yet about the ball, or has he been neglectful?" she asked as they drew closer.

"He has asked," LaVet confirmed.

"What do you think of the idea?" She looked from Lady Maren to Kenric before venturing an answer.

"I believe a ball would be very well received."

"There is more, isn't there? You're holding back." Lady Maren squinted up at her.

"No, it's just that... well it's still unsuitably warm for a ball."

"A picnic it is then!" Lady Maren smiled and went back to her tea.

"Well, now that it's been decided I will leave the details to the experts." Kenric bowed and turned to leave.

"You will not go without taking your leave, Kenric?" Lady Maren asked.

"No, Grandmother, I am only off to discuss a few last minute details with my steward. I would never venture to depart without allowing the two of you to shower me with 'return soon' and 'safe travels', etcetera, etcetera and so forth."

"Give Gallagher my regards." Lady Maren said as a farewell, watching him leave she sighed. "I do so hate to have him away so much," then seeming to notice that LaVet was still near by, "Would you take some tea with me, my dear?"

"I have not yet changed out of my riding habit."

"We will not stand upon ceremony today; please keep an old women in company."

The butler pulled out a chair for LaVet and she sank into it.

"So, how are you, my dear?"

"I am well. How are you, Lady Maren? I feel as though we have been so engaged with diversions for our guest that we have had little time to talk these past few days."

Lady Maren assented, "I am always sad to see Kenric leave but I can not say the same for Sir Fitzroy. The sooner he departs for London, the easier I will rest." She sipped at her tea then, placing her cup down, smiled at LaVet. "I am pleased that Kenric has asked to present you as his wife to our acquaintances. I know you are already well known in Tredan for your charity visits with Pastor Long's wife. But this is a pleasure I was sure Kenric would forego for some time, due to the nature of your marriage. It says much of his high regard for you to wish to present you so soon."

"I am very sensible of the honor. I only wish to uphold the great Leighton name and not fall short of his-- or your expectations of me."

"Impossible!" Lady Maren snapped. "I have the utmost faith in you and anyone with half a wit will love you instantly, as I did."

LaVet was unable to stop an image of Kenric from distracting her mind, and she wondered what on earth *he* must think of *her*.

~ Chapter Five~

"Lady Leighton, you are the very spirit of generosity."

LaVet flushed and shook her head. "Mrs. Long, you are too kind and liberal with your compliments," she countered as the two walked down the lane leading from the chapel to the main road.

"No! I cannot tell you how blessed we are by your benevolence! Donating so much fine clothe to the ladies of our congregation to fashion clothes and quilts from, for the poor, was more than I could have ever hoped for. We have never had so much bounty before to distribute to those in need. I feel quite overwhelmed by the outpouring of true Christian charity you bestow upon all those around you daily.

"My husband informed me just this morning that he saw you taking food in to Mrs. Blakeslee and her children. I simply cannot tell you what a kindness that is. It is sincerely touching."

LaVet was glad when Mrs. Long stopped her high praise to take a breath, allowing a chance to change the subject. "Is it true that the chapel will soon be fitted for a new pipe organ?"

"Indeed! I cannot tell you how delighted we are with the prospect. We raised the funds over quite a long period and it will finally be installed just before Christmas is upon us. There is nothing better than a full congregation singing hymns of praise with the accompaniment of a fine instrument, don't you agree?"

LaVet wasn't sure that Mrs. Long really wanted to know if she did or didn't agree because she continued speaking as they walked.

As the two women neared the carriage waiting to whisk LaVet home, Mrs. Long slowed her step and turned to face LaVet.

Catching up both of LaVet's hands in hers, she smiled at her warmly. "I cannot tell you how blessed we are to have you as the mistress of Leighton Manor. You have breathed new life into the old manor house and the tenant farms, as well as Tredan. You are a godsend and I am grateful for you beyond words."

"Mrs. Long, it is I that am grateful to be here and for the chance of service." LaVet made her farewells with her and moved to the carriage. The door was opened for her and LaVet stepped inside.

As the door was being fastened behind her Mrs. Long called out, "Give my kindest regards to Lady Maren."

Lady Maren had chosen to ride with LaVet but refused to exit the carriage. She now pulled up the screen and peered out at Mrs. Long.

"Will I have the pleasure of seeing you and your husband at the picnic?"

For a moment Mrs. Long seemed a bit flustered, then with a large grin she nodded.

"Oh yes, I cannot tell you how pleased we were to receive the invitation. We are both looking forward to such a pleasant diversion, I cannot tell you."

"Very good." Lady Maren interrupted the stream of complimentary statements still pouring out from Mrs. Long. "I beg your leave, Mrs. Long. I am feeling the lateness of the day."

With a wave she snapped the screen back into place and tapped her cane on the roof, signaling the driver to leave.

"Lady Maren, I've never known you to be abrupt with anyone besides Kenric before. Do you dislike Mrs. Long?" LaVet asked as the carriage rattled away.

"Oh, I like Mrs. Long just fine, my dear. She is a good woman and does a great deal of great charity work. I do, however, have a difficult time when talking to her. She begins every sentence with the phrase, 'I cannot tell you,' then promptly proceeds to tell you what she just professed she could not! It is only made tolerable to stomach because she is such a fine Christian woman."

LaVet openly laughed. "You are being unjust," she accused.

"I suppose you are right," Lady Maren sighed.

LaVet smiled at her. "I do enjoy her company and enthusiasm for life. She is a great talker; I'll allow that. However, Mrs. Long is also an exceptional woman with many great talents that she uses to benefit others. It is hard to find fault in such a person."

"I have been rightly chastised for my rudeness," Lady Maren said. "Perhaps I should try harder to overlook her excessive speaking."

"Thank you for riding into Tredan with me today. I find I hate to travel alone in a carriage." LaVet smiled at the older women.

"Of course my dear. Although I must confess it was purely a selfish act. I have become so accustomed to your company that I am loath to forego it."

***

"I believe that is enough." Kenric pushed the tankard of mead from Fitzroy's reach.

"Damn it man, why would you come between a man and his drink?" Fitzroy bellowed loudly.

"Come, Fitz, you'll feel better after a night's rest." Kenric took his friend by the arm and coaxed him from the chair, and with faltering footsteps led him to the room in the Inn which Fitzroy had procured for the night.

Fitzroy staggered over to the bed and lay prone on his chest, mumbling, "What has she done to me... I loved her."

"Sleep now. Things will look clearer in the morning," Kenric said and left the room.

As he returned to the ruckus of the tavern Kenric noted the entrance of several members of Her Majesty's Royal Navy.

"Kenric?" His name was called by someone in the center of the confusion, and it took him several moments to find a recognizable face.

"Barton! Barton Roche." The two clasped hands and slapped each other on the back. "It is good to see you."

"You are the last person I thought I would run into here." Barton laughed. "Is my sister with you?"

"No, I am not in town for pleasure," Kenric said regrettably.

"Are you leaving or would you care to join me for a drink?" Barton asked.

"I have had my fill of drinking, but I will join you." The two sat at a nearly empty table and Barton ordered food before they returned to their conversation.

"So tell me, Kenric, how is Little Bit? Giving you all kinds of trouble, I should think?"

"Little Bit?"

Barton laughed, "My name for her. She hated it so much as a child that I hardly ever called her anything else."

"She is fine, or was when I left. I'm afraid that my information is almost a month old."

"Your business in London is taking quite a while then?"

"Longer than I had hoped, to be sure. I am happy to say it is concluded and I will be on my way home in the morning."

"Then I am lucky to have stumbled across you." Barton reached into his breast pocket and retrieved a letter. "I was going to post this. Would you mind delivering it for me instead?" He pushed the letter toward Kenric.

"I am sure she will be delighted to receive it." Kenric gladly took the letter.

"How is married life treating you?" Barton questioned, as his food was set before him.

Kenric hesitated. "Well…"

Barton threw back his head and laughed heartily. "She *is* giving you trouble, isn't she? I am partly to blame for that, I suppose. I always did encourage her."

"No, your sister has been quite… wonderful." Kenric wasn't able to stop the image of LaVet that flashed through his mind.

"She must be behaving herself. I suppose the several-- and I do mean several-- warnings she received from father to conduct herself in a manner befitting a lady finally sank in." Barton laughed and took a large bite of his supper.

"All right, now you have gained my interest."

***

Lady Maren excused herself to lie down before dressing for dinner. Finding herself with a few unoccupied hours, LaVet retired to the music room. Drawing open the heavy curtains to allow the sunlight to stream into the space, she seated herself on the stool for the pedal harp and began to pluck at the strings.

Each note rang clearly in the room. Soon her fingers were flying; the individual notes cascading as the song floated out from the harp to fill the air around her. Closing her eyes, she felt each crescendo washing away the stress and loneliness of the past weeks. A weight she hadn't realized she carried lifted off her shoulders as the last tones of the song faded into memory.

"You played that piece exceedingly well." LaVet's eyes flew open as reality crashed down about her again.

"I didn't realize I had an audience," she said, and turned in her seat to face Collingwood.

"It has been sometime since music has graced this home. Your presence is a very pleasant change." He bowed to her.

"Thank you, Mr. Collingwood, the compliment is greatly appreciated." LaVet got to her feet then asked, "Is there something I can help you with?"

"Lord Leighton has sent word that he is returning this evening. He will meet with Gallagher then join you and Lady Maren at dinner."

"Thank you for informing me." Collingwood exited with a small nod.

LaVet paced the floor a few times as a bundle of nerves settled in her middle. Feeling a desperate need for air, she left the house to wander the gardens. She had been in anticipation of Kenric's return for days; however, the knowledge that her husband was now on his way made her strangely uneasy, and brought feelings she wasn't aware she even had close to the surface.

Her footsteps took her to the edge of manicured lawns and clipped hedges. Staying close to the tree line she wandered for the larger part of the afternoon, attempting to sort out her feelings as they swung wildly between uneasiness and eagerness.

As the sun dipped lower in the sky she knew it was time for her to return and dress for dinner. As she approached the manor LaVet smiled to see Frances coming into the garden to meet her.

"Miss, what have you done to your petticoats!" Frances gasped at the sight of LaVet, who looked down and saw layers of dirt and brambles clinging to the bottom of the skirts.

"Why is it, miss, that so often I am left to mend ruined gowns and scrub mountains' worth of dirt from them?" Frances asked, as she strode toward the house with LaVet in tow. "What on earth have you been doing?"

"I just went for a simple walk at the edge of the wood."

Frances scoffed, "Nothing with you is simple, miss."

"Frances, are you happy here?"

"I could do without the extra challenges you present me with, miss but yes, I am happy."

"I am glad to hear it," LaVet said in earnest.

"Are you unhappy, miss? Has something happened to distress you?" Frances asked.

LaVet found she wasn't able to answer the question honestly to herself or Frances.

"I am not unhappy," she finally answered.

"You must be glad the master is home," Frances was saying as they reached LaVet's chambers.

LaVet couldn't respond. It didn't seem to matter to Frances who talked until it was time for LaVet to step into the bath and ready herself for dinner.

"Shall I lay out your green dress for tonight miss? It is Lord Leighton's favorite color." Frances said with a knowing smile.

LaVet wanted to ask her maid how she could possibly know what Kenric's favorite color was, when she herself had no idea. LaVet sank deeply into the perfumed water and tried to relax.

Frances set to work washing LaVet's hair and sooner than LaVet thought possible she was gazing at her reflection in the mirror. The velvet green dress was stunning and cut in the latest style. The richness of its color brightened the emerald green of her eyes and deepened the richness of her raven hair.

***

Kenric stood when LaVet entered the dining room. He regarded her closely and his gaze shone with appreciation when their eyes met.

Stepping around the table he strode to her side, "You look lovely," he smiled.

"Thank you," she replied, and took the arm offered. Kenric guided her to her chair and pulled it out for her. She noted that Lady Maren was still absent from the table, and that her place had not been set.

"Won't your grandmother be joining us?"

"She isn't feeling well and is taking supper in her room tonight," he answered as the first course was served.

"I am sorry to hear that," LaVet said with concern. "I do hope she is feeling better soon, I will miss her company."

Each fell into silence, and after few attempts to eat past the lump in her throat, LaVet lay down her spoon and sipped at her wine instead.

"You don't care for cream of barley?" Kenric asked.

"No, the soup is fine," she assured him, and endeavored to take another sip.

"I had the opportunity of speaking with my steward upon my arrival. He was very complimentary in regards to you," Kenric observed.

"Oh?"

"Yes; I was instructed to ask you about an incident between Ramus Mossop and Nicholls Crane?" Kenric motioned for the dishes to be cleared and the next course brought out.

Plates of poached salmon with mousseline sauce and cucumbers appeared before them.

"I did not realize that my... counsel on the matter impressed your steward enough that it might prove a topic of conversation," she said, as a rush of color touched her cheeks. Her hand flew to the necklace and rubbed the stone lightly.

"It must have been some feat. Gallagher does not often shower praise. I have been held in suspense long enough; please, do enlighten me." Kenric smiled at her, his food forgotten.

"It was a trifle really. As you know, Mr. Mossop owns a fine drove of cattle. Mr. Crane also owns several head, although not nearly the same amount. One of Mr. Mossop's kine went missing. It was discovered later that it was sent to slaughter with one other of Mr. Crane's, purely on accident.

"Mr. Mossop would not accept the beef and an apology. It was demanded that Mr. Crane right the wrong by paying the full price of the animal in question-- immediately."

Kenric sat back in his seat. "I know both of these men. There is no possible way that Crane would have those kinds of funds at his disposal."

"True, and neither side would budge and soon your mediation was called upon as the land owner. When it was discovered that you were still away from home, Henry was asked to hear them out."

"How then did you become involved?" He pressed.

"As negotiations became heated I... intervened."

"Intervened?"

LaVet looked from her untouched salmon to Kenric; he was watching her closely.

"I proposed a new method of payment for Mr. Mossop that was agreeable to both parties," she said, then expounded further, "Mr. Mossop is quite a bit older than Mr. Crane. He has no sons and must hire out for help with his large number of cattle. Mr. Crane has five sons. It made sense to point out the obvious solution.

"Mr. Crane's eldest son, Taylor, will go and work for Mr. Mossop until the debt has been paid. The Crane family gladly accepted the chance to keep some of the best cuts of beef; the rest will be sold and any profits will be returned to Mr. Mossop. I also suggested that the first order of business for Taylor would be to mend the fence between his father's cattle and those of their neighbor."

"I can see I left things well in hand. Nicely settled."

She shook her head a little, brushing aside the praise. "It was the only logical solution."

"With so much happening when I returned it slipped my mind to tell you-- I was able to see your brother. He sent you this." Kenric reached into his breast pocket and retrieved a letter.

"Barton!" she exclaimed happily, and took the small folded paper as it was offered to her.

"Yes, he was traveling through London and it was purely by chance that we crossed paths."

"Were you able to spend any time with him?" she asked.

"Yes, I was able to share a meal with your brother who, I might add, was more than happy to provide me with many details of your young life together." Kenric was smiling widely now.

LaVet flushed, "My brother is prone to exaggeration."

Kenric turned his eyes to her and one eyebrow lifted. "Are you saying that you cannot hunt better than most men? Is that an exaggeration?"

"That should not be shocking; it is not a talent exclusive to men," she pointed out.

"Then, you do enjoy the hunt?" he inquired.

"I am proficient with a bow," she acknowledged.

"And the gun; so I hear."

She laughed, "Barton is a very poor shot and I know of many who would be able to best him."

"Then his exaggeration must be in your ability with a sword," he commented with a wicked grin.

LaVet sat for several long moments before attempting an answer.

"Against my father's wishes, Barton encouraged my more boisterous nature and invited me to become his sparring partner."

"Against your father's wishes?" Kenric pressed.

"My mother and sister were model genteel females. I was wild, and displeased him almost daily with my inclination for unladylike sport." LaVet allowed her eyes to drop.

"I feel I have been duped," Kenric said in a mockingly shocked manner.

"How so?"

"I was led to believe I married a gentlewomen. You have hidden your wildness well," he said with a testing smile. "Although, thinking back, there have been a few times your strong opinion *has* reared its head."

"Heaven forbid! A woman with a strong opinion!" she said with wide eyes, covering her mouth with one hand, feigning shock. Kenric laughed and sat forward. LaVet instantly felt more at ease with him; more like herself.

"Yes, growing up with the likes of Lady Maren certainly did not prepare me for a life of strong opinions." He leaned toward her. "Why did I have to learn about these very intriguing topics from your brother?"

"Perhaps I have not yet been comfortable enough to show my true nature, or had the opportunity. I would not want you to profoundly regret your choice in a bride so soon, Sir. True unhappiness in our marriage is still a few years off," she said playfully.

"I, for one, would have comfortably yourself at all times." He glanced at her then added, "Regardless of who is in your company."

"You may come to regret that statement," she warned. "I believe my father was very glad to broker peace between our families and supporters; yet, he may have been equally happy to be rid of me, as troublesome as I am."

"Marriage is the span of life in which the parts of ourselves we keep hidden from the rest of the world come pouring out into the open between husband and wife. There is no way to hide our true selves, and it is pointless attempting it."

"So you do not mind a wife who can ride and shoot as well as a man? One who openly speaks her own mind even if it is in direct disagreement with you?"

"Well, I suppose that depends," he answered, looking thoughtful.

"On?"

"How well you can wield a sword." The corners of his lips turned upward slightly.

~ Chapter Six ~

LaVet arose well before the sun and was combing out and pinning her own hair before her maid came in to draw the curtains and attend to her.

"Good morning Lady Leighton, I trust you slept well."

"Yes, Frances I did." LaVet smiled to herself. She had eaten no more than a few bites of her dinner the previous evening and yet could not remember a more pleasant meal.

Frances took over pinning up LaVet's hair and the two sat chatting warmly, as old friends.

"What do you think, will it do?" Frances asked as LaVet surveyed the finished arrangement.

"You are quite talented, Frances. I am lucky to have you."

"Thank you. Now you'd better hurry down to breakfast." Frances cast her a sly smirk in the mirror.

The breakfast room was empty when LaVet entered. Before taking her seat she walked to the tall windows, early morning sun spilling in through them, and looked outside. The day was bright and clear.

"Good morning." Kenric's whispered greeting came from just behind her. He was so close, in fact, that when LaVet spun to look at him she collided into him. Her hands shot outward to stop a fall. It wasn't until she had regained sure footing that she realized her hands were now pressed to his chest. She pulled them back as if her fingers had been on fire.

Dismay must have shown clearly on her face as their eyes met; but Kenric showed no sign of sharing the emotion.

"How are you this morning?" he asked.

There was nothing that could be done about the pink in her cheeks or the lack of air in her lungs. He was so close, so near to her that it was intoxicating and she took a step back to look at him with any degree of comfort.

"LaVet? Are you all right?" Pulling herself back into the moment she blinked a few times, as if coming out of a trance.

"Yes, I'm sorry... I was lost in thought. Forgive me, what were you saying?" she managed to stammer.

"I was asking how you were... are you well?" It was almost impossible for her to think with his nearness.

"I am well," she reassured him.

"Would you feel up to accompanying me on a ride this morning?" Kenric asked, leading her to the table with his hands pressed to the small of her back, guiding her.

"I would, my Lord," LaVet answered happily.

Kenric pulled out her chair and then sat to her right, at the head of the table. "There is one condition we must discuss first," he said, reaching for a plate heavy with cheese and fruit.

"A condition, my Lord?"

"Yes. You see, I have always used your given name, "LaVet", when I address you. Yet, after months of marriage you still address me in the formal, "my Lord". I would have you call me by my given name."

"That is your condition to my going riding with you?"

"It is."

"I agree to your terms, my Lord--" She stopped and suppressed a smile, "It will be hard habit for me to overcome, I'm afraid." With his eyes on her face she formed his name on her lips, saying it aloud for the first time. "Kenric."

He was smiling brightly at her now. "Much better."

"What little secret are the two of you sharing that has made both of you smile so?" Lady Maren asked, as she entered the breakfast room.

"I am taking LaVet riding this morning, grandmother," Kenric said, as he stood and helped her into her seat then reclaimed his own.

"I'm glad to hear it," she said, then added, "She needs a bit of fun. I noticed in your absence these last three weeks something of a dark cloud has fallen over your wife. I watched her take many a long walk alone around the garden, and spend hours confined in your dusty library or studying the family portraits in the hall." Lady Maren talked about her as if LaVet was not seated across the table, mortified by the information Lady Maren was offering.

"Really? What do you account for the change in her demeanor grandmother?" Kenric asked, looking right at LaVet.

"She was very sullen after the departure of her father and brother. I thought that might be it; perhaps a touch of homesickness. Added to this your constant absence from home..." she stuttered a little. "Your return could not be more welcome to either of us, I can tell you that."

"I am glad to be back," he said simply, his gaze never leaving LaVet's face.

"You will be yourself again now, my dear, now that Kenric is home," Lady Maren said with a sympathetic smile at LaVet. "You must make a day of it, Kenric," she added as the idea hit her, reached out to touch his arm in emphasis.

"Do you think so?" he asked.

"Oh yes! Have cook prepare a luncheon and picnic in that pretty glen... you know the one I mean?"

"I believe I do," he agreed. "What you say LaVet; how do you regard this prospect?"

"I would like nothing better," she said in honesty. The look he then gave her sent her pulse racing.

"Good." Kenric turned his attention to Lady Maren. "How are you feeling this morning, grandmother? I would not feel right leaving if you are still unwell."

"I do believe the heat of yesterday's ride in the carriage made me overly tired. I feel much better today."

"Then it's settled. Ronald, please ask cook to pack a picnic lunch for Lady Leighton and I? Let her know we would like to leave as soon as we are done breakfasting, thank you." The young footman that had been refreshing the sideboard nodded diligently and rushed from the room.

***

"The woods are more extensive than I expected," LaVet commented as they rode. "I did not realize on the day we met that I was already on your property. I supposed the greater portion of the estate to be farmland."

"My mother loved long rides along these very trails. My father found joy in seeking her happiness, so he had large tracts of the forest on his land preserved for her singular enjoyment," Kenric explained.

"He must have loved your mother very much," she observed.

"And she him. When my father died suddenly she was shattered from the loss and slipped from this world not long after. I've always believed her heart just stopped beating, without his companionship."

The sentiment was sadly beautiful and it pained LaVet to think of it. Kenric spoke no more of his parents but rode on, the songs of birds the only sound. After a few long minutes he turned to her and reined in his horse.

As they drew up he pointed into the distance. "Right over there is where I saw you for the first time."

She looked in the direction and could see nothing distinctive to mark the area. "How can you be sure?"

"There are some moments in one's life that are not easily forgotten."

She was unable to look at Kenric; her emotions became tussled at his words. In order to force them back into a more manageable state she kept her eyes on the distant trees and tried to memorize their shapes.

"Shall we continue?" he asked, after a moment. LaVet could not find her voice to comment, and Kenric went on by asking, "How have you enjoyed your time whilst I was away?"

"With every passing hour I have fallen more in love with all the differing parts of this beautiful place. I had an instant liking for Tredan and those who live there. I look forward to my time with Mrs. Long as well; she is a charming woman and has taken me to many of the farms surrounding Tredan in our travels."

"And how do you like Leighton Manor?"

"There is certainly nothing there to complain of. I would be honored to present it as my home to anyone of my acquaintance. Although, I do still lose myself in its maze of rooms from time to time," she admitted.

"The servants? Are they kind to you?" he pressed.

"Again, there is no fault to find," she answered. "May I ask to what purpose these questions tend?"

"I am trying to discern what grandmother could have perceived that betrayed such deep unhappiness in you, and thus find a remedy." His look was searching.

"Any unhappiness she perceived was solely self-imposed. Do not let it trouble you any further."

"When two people marry they are become tied together by the strings of fate. If something happens to one it is inevitable that it will affect the other," Kenric said.

"It is a nice sentiment, which might be true of those who genuinely share their lives. I'm afraid that in our case, being so continuously apart-- distant in more than geographies-- it does not apply," she whispered, shocked by her boldness. "Oh, I apologize for my frankness."

"No, you are right. How can we ever become friendly if I am forever from home. It is for that reason that I turned down the opportunity for further business ventures in London with Fitzroy. He was disappointed; yet I have the feeling he will recover soon."

LaVet looked at him in surprise. "You turned him down?"

"Seeing your brother helped me to make the decision. He is… a very persuasive man, Barton." Kenric gave her a half smile.

"Why do I have the feeling that you discussed much more with my dear brother than I would entirely approve of?"

"He merely pointed out my great error in judgment."

"A talent of Barton's I know well," LaVet laughed. "May I inquire after the nature of this error?" Their eyes met and held.

"Leaving Leighton Manor," Kenric said simply.

"I do wish you weren't as absent from home as you have been." Again she was shocked by her own openness.

"Then I will make a cautious effort to remain home as much as my duties will allow." Kenric didn't continue the subject and she was glad of it; not ready to focus on the emotions battling within her. LaVet cast her eyes forward to the trail but could feel his gaze on her from time to time as they slowly rode on.

They rambled for several minutes this way before Kenric slowed his horse.

"Is there a problem?" LaVet asked.

"This is where we must tether the horses," he said, and dismounted. Kenric made his way to her side and with his hands at her waist he lifted her down from her mount, setting her on her feet. Moving to gather the reins of her horse, his fingers brushed hers as he slid then from her grasp.

After tying the horses to a sturdy tree and giving each a bit of carrot he kept in a saddlebag. Kenric untied the bag containing their lunch. Laying a blanket over one arm, he turned back to face her.

"This way," he said and started a slow walk deeper under the canopy of the trees.

"My great-grandfather came upon this meadow, and it soon became a favorite spot for the family. We have discovered that many in the town have found their way here, but beyond our borders it is a secret; a place preserved for only those living near."

The trees grew closer together, forcing her to walk behind him on the winding path through the low hanging branches.

The trail inclined sharply over a rise and Kenric offered LaVet his hand. She took it, despite her sure footing, and noted with a smile that when the ground leveled out again he made no move to release her from his grasp.

Soon the trees thinned and she took in a sharp breath in wonder at the sight before her.

"I never imagined it would look quite like this," she said in awe. It was not a extensive area but almost every inch was carpeted with blooming wildflowers, vibrantly colored so vibrant and alive. Cutting its way through the sea of reds, purples, yellows and blues was a thin, laughing trickle of water. The meadow was bright and warm even in the shadows being cast over its edges by the surrounding trees.

"What do you think?" he asked.

"It's magnificent," she answered, lifting her face to look at him. "Thank you for sharing it with me."

Kenric eyes held LaVet's as he smiled down at her. "I'm pleased you like it."

Still holding her hand, he led her to a level spot where the flowers were sparse and laid out the blanket he had brought with him. LaVet took the lunch prepared for them from his hands and spread it as Kenric stretched out next to her.

As they ate LaVet attempted several times to start a conversation, but each time she opened her mouth the words didn't seem to come to her. Then Kenric broke the silence. "I brought you something from London."

"Something more than Barton's letter?" LaVet said, intrigued.

"Yes." Kenric sat forward and revealed a brown paper wrapped parcel, so small it was easy to conceal in the palm of his hand.

LaVet plucked it from his fingers and with careful movements unwrapped a jeweled brooch. Various jewels of purple, green and blue winked at her from the setting that mimicked the eye of a peacock feather.

"I appreciate your sense of humor," she laughed at him, smiling broadly.

"I didn't intend for it to be a joke. You are hard not to notice… even if you do not wish to be."

~ Chapter Seven ~

"Good afternoon, grandmother." Kenric placed a kiss on her cheek.

"Yes it is, and how are you, my dear boy?" She looked up from her seat to gauge his response.

"Very well." He noticed the disordered papers resting in front of her on the tabletop. "What has you so occupied?"

"LaVet asked me to review plans for the picnic. I believe she is slightly overwhelmed with it all." Lady Maren chortled. "Although I do not blame her. The first public introduction after a marriage is always a bit trying." To emphasize her words Lady Maren nodded to the large window near her writing desk.

Kenric went to it. "How long has she been wandering the gardens?"

"All morning," Lady Maren sighed, as she joined Kenric.

"She often seems sad." Kenric observed with a heavy heart.

"Marriage is very different for a woman. We are asked to leave everything behind except what will fit in a trunk. Leaving friends, family, places and people we have known and loved our whole lives to become a fixture in the life of our husbands. While, in most cases, the husband's daily life changes little." Lady Maren patted Kenric's hand.

"LaVet has been displaced and must come to know herself in a different light, that of *your* wife. Although I believe she is doing a fine job adjusting to the demands made on her as Lady of Leighton Manor... there is much expected of her in that respect and it can all can be very daunting. Other adjustments may be harder to make, and for a woman with a... free spirit such as hers..."

"Was it as hard for you to adjust once you and grandfather were married?" Kenric was listening with a growing sense of trepidation. The last thing he wanted was for LaVet to be unhappy.

"It is impossible to compare. I was the eldest daughter and was instructed by my mother from a young age to run a large household. Your grandfather and I courted for many months before our marriage took place, as well. LaVet had a very different experience."

Kenric watched as LaVet sat on one of the garden benches.

"Grandmother… I know you find her company pleasing, but do you *like* her? I mean… really like her?" Kenric asked with real interest.

"I don't think that I am indeed the one who should be answering that question."

He stood unmoving, his eyes locked on the far figure, "I fear that I've done something irreversible, and fallen in love with her without being aware it was even happening."

"That is how love works. It is not often loud or boisterous. Under the right circumstances it… grows, and can continue to do so for a lifetime," Lady Maren mused.

Kenric leaned one arm on the sill of the window and pressed his forehead to a glass pane. "I had no idea it would feel like… like *this*, this living thing inside of me that hungers for her. I find everything about her fascinating… her conversation captivating, her presence intoxicating.

"When I am around her I feel as though there is no better use of my time than to make her smile. When I am away from her I can't seem to remove her from my thoughts. I live in agony, not knowing… if she could ever return my affection."

"You will know when it is the right time to tell her of your feelings, and I have no doubt of her returning them."

Kenric made no answer. Allowing himself to speak the words aloud, to admit that what he felt for her had developed far beyond what he believed possible had been difficult, but to entertain the wish that she would welcome his affection-- or return it-- almost seemed too much to hope for.

His grandmother seemed to understand his need for solitude and returned to her desk. Kenric gazed out the window for several minutes longer, watching as her lady's maid came out and conversed with LaVet for several minutes on a topic that seemed to enthrall them both. When she was left alone again she took to walking about the expansive grounds. Kenric watched her receding figure for only a few seconds before his own footsteps led him outdoors.

***

LaVet stood just inside the open terrace doors, her eyes searching the crowd as their guests gathered in the gardens of the manor house. Kenric stepped up next to her. LaVet smoothed her new summer frock out in nervousness.

"You look lovely," he said, inspecting her closely. "The brooch is a nice touch. It looks lovely with your mother's necklace."

LaVet clasped her necklace for a moment, taking strength from her mother's memory. "Thank you."

Kenric put her at ease with a smile and she returned it, and then touched the jeweled pin. "I thought you would appreciate my wearing the brooch."

"Shall we?" he asked, and offered her his arm.

LaVet was only able to nod her assent as she took Kenric's arm and together they walked from the house. All eyes turned to them as they descended the stone staircase and into the throng of people awaiting them.

LaVet was introduced to person after person. Gentlemen kissed her hand, women bowed and each wished her well and expressed happiness over their marriage. Kenric stood close by as the procession of well-wishers passed by.

Kenric stepped in after a time to claim his wife from their guests and whisked her away, gently placing a hand on her back to guide her. Taking her hand, he led her to a seat with the Long's and took his place next to her. Heavily-laden platters of meats, cheeses and fruits were served. The hum of chatter and activity died down as the food was consumed under the comfortable shade provided by a maze of tents.

After only a few bites of her lunch Mrs. Long turned to Kenric, and with her face alight with animation began speaking to him, "Lord Leighton, I don't believe that my dear husband and I have expressed to you our gratitude for all the work and acts of generosity your wife has shown the parishioners of our congregation. Upon your departure to London she dove right in to working closely with myself and the ladies of the aid society.

"Seeing to the sick, caring for the invalids and widows-- showing such Christian charity as I have never known. I do believe I saw her doing one or another act of pure kindness nearly every day. I found myself seeking her counsel on many occasions. You have brought among us an angel."

LaVet felt embarrassment flushing her skin at the high praise and wanted to protest, knowing in her heart that she had filled her time with charitable work in order to keep her mind off the fact as a new bride she had been left alone.

"I have heard many favorable reports regarding her actions in my absence," Kenric agreed. "I thank you for yours."

"This is quite literally the best punch I have ever had." Mrs. Long paused to sip at her cup. "I cannot tell you how much Mr. Long and I looked forward to picnic. It was simply a wonderful idea and we are honored to have been invited. And how fortuitous to have had it on such an absolutely perfect day! There is the slightest of breezes to keep everyone quite comfortable, and I dare say, I have never seen an equal to this magnificent lunch being served," she gushed.

Kenric was only able to give Mrs. Long a passive smile before the woman continued.

"Now, tell me if I am wrong, but I did hear through tittle tattle, as it were, that we will have further diversions with games of croquet, hoops, shuttlecock and nine pins!" Mrs. Long stressed the name of each game in her excitement.

"You are quite right, Mrs. Long. We may also play a few rounds of blind man's bluff, if you would honor us with taking the turn," Kenric declared, bestowing on her his most dazzling smile.

"Oh! I do love a good game of blind man's bluff," she clapped.

"I thought you might," he laughed.

"It is a pity that Lady Abney is still visiting her relations," Mrs. Long said, her face instantly sorrowful as she turned to LaVet. "She is quite good at blind man's bluff and I know of no one who takes more pleasure in merriment. You have not yet made her acquaintance. Yet, I am certain the two of you will become fast friends."

"I was informed that her father's estate is an easy distance from Leighton Manor, and I do hope to call upon her when she returns from Bath," LaVet promised.

Lady Maren, who had taken her lunch in the comfort of the house, appeared.

"Dear Mrs. Long, I would like to take a turn about the garden before the games begin, would you mind accompanying me?"

Mrs. Long rose hastily to her feet, the remains of her lunch instantly forgotten. "It would be my pleasure Lady Maren. Thank you for asking." Linking her arm with Lady Maren, the two moved off from the larger assembled body.

LaVet watched them go before returning to her own food. Kenric was in conversation with Mr. Long. All the others that surrounded her were also pleasantly engaged in discussing a variety of topics.

After it seemed the eating had slowed down Kenric announced that the games would be set up forthwith, while tea and cakes were served. He then thanked them all for coming to help celebrate his marriage. LaVet felt heat rush to her face as many dozens of eyes turned toward her.

Holding out his hand Kenric pulled her to her feet, "Which diversion would you like to partake in first?"

"You have found the weak link in my armor. I am not much for games and have never had a talent for them," she protested.

"How can that be? I cannot believe you would but excel at any endeavor," he said with a wicked grin.

"You give me far too much credit for something you have not yet observed," she countered.

"Enlighten me." Kenric offered her his arm.

"What shall we play?" She asked and linked her arm through his.

"How do you feel about a game of shuttlecock?"

"Perfectly awful," she responded.

***

"Would you care to join us?" Lady Maren pressed LaVet who had shut her book, marking her place with a ribbon. LaVet looked at Kenric and Lady Maren seated at a card table and wasn't able to refrain from wrinkling her nose.

"No, Grandmother. My wife has no taste for games and detests them in all their forms," he said, his voice matter of fact.

Lady Maren lifted an eyebrow. "Does he speak the truth?"

"Your grandson is teasing me," LaVet reassured Lardy Maren.

"And why should he?"

"Because at the picnic he shamed me by beating me horribly at every game. I was forced to find refuge on the swing to avoid the constant humiliation of being undone at every turn."

"Kenric! It is a very unattractive quality in a man to be so competitive with one of the weaker sex," Lady Maren reprimanded him.

"Do not be too hard on him. I am quite ridiculous at games," LaVet laughed, placing her book on the side table. "Yet, I am determined to improve my skill so I might be able to provide my husband with a more challenging opponent in the future. For now,

I am tired and must beg your forgiveness as I take my leave." She stood and placed a tender kiss on the cheek of Lady Maren.

"Good night, my dear," Lady Maren smiled.

"Would you like me to escort you?" Kenric asked, as he pushed his chair back and stood.

"Please, stay and finish your hand," LaVet pressed.

"Nonsense, he will escort you," Lady Maren stated, and placed her hand of cards on the table as punctuation.

LaVet, unable to argue the point, took his arm and allowed him to lead her from the room.

"Did you enjoy yourself today?" Kenric asked, as they took the stairs.

"Yes, I was glad to meet those of your acquaintance who I have not had the opportunity to meet before. And you? How do you feel it went?"

"You were very well received, although that was never in question. I knew that all who that had the chance to meet you would be taken with you." LaVet felt a flutter in her middle at the compliment.

Kenric cleared his throat and continued when she made no response, "In my observations I learned something new about you today."

"Pray, tell?"

"You once told me you were honest to a fault. The only way to prove such a statement is to put it to the test. At first I was convinced you were just being modest, but I am now of the mind to believe you were right... you *are* utterly dreadful at games."

LaVet burst out laughing, then once she regained her composure commented, "I feel so unlike myself when being watched. I suppose it is for that reason I have never excelled at games or wanted to try. It would draw attention, and that was my last wish. Perhaps that also explains my propensity to indulge in things considered to be unladylike. As long as my father didn't approve of my talents I would never be asked to display them."

"It is an interesting theory, although it doesn't account for your extensive musical abilities."

"Who would call on the younger daughter when the elder is far superior a talent?" she questioned.

"In any case, I am glad you had an agreeable time."

"I did. Thank you." They had reached her chambers and she slipped her hand from his arm.

Turning to face her he gave a slight bow. "Sleep well, LaVet."

"Good night, Kenric," she whispered, and then catching sight of the tempest that raged in the depths of his eyes was momentarily frozen to the spot.

It seemed for several long moments that Kenric wished to add something to their conversation. His lips parted then closed, forming a thin line; his eyes never leaving hers.

"Good night." He said finally, and turning on his heel he retreated down the hall.

~ Chapter Eight ~

LaVet was setting her pen down next to the unfinished letter to her father when a knock came at the sitting room door. Turning to see Collingwood she nodded.

"Is everything all right?"

"You have a visitor, ma'am. Lady Abney has come to call on you. Shall I show her in?"

LaVet took in a sharp breath, "Yes, Collingwood. Thank you."

Before he was able to announce her, a finely dressed woman swept her way into the room. LaVet took stock of her in an instant: tall, shapely, with the most perfect complexion she had ever seen. LaVet felt herself shrink back as Lady Abney's deep blue eyes, piercing and shrewd, swept everything in the room then landed promptly on LaVet with a clear air of condescension.

"Lady Leighton, may I introduce Lady Emmaleen Abney." Collingwood bowed and departed the sitting room.

LaVet curtsied. "You are very welcome, Lady Abney."

Lady Abney returned the gesture and both women sat across from each other.

"It is such a pleasure to meet the new mistress of Leighton Manor."

"Thank you Lady Abney, I am truly honored by your visit. How did you like Bath?"

"Bath in season is always wonderful, but I am glad to be home. So many things have changed during my absence that I hardly recognize it."

"I would have called on you if news of your return had reached us. I apologize for any slight in the matter." LaVet rushed to say, praying that Lady Abney's clear coldness was due to some misunderstanding that could easily be reminded.

Lady Abney gave LaVet an appraising look and still seemed as though she wasn't at all happy with what she saw.

Now unsure of what to say, LaVet complimented her on her lovely dress and asked her how her trip was. For several painful minutes they attempted more small talk.

Suddenly Lady Abney stood and took a turn around the room. "I have often spent a pleasant time in this very space. I am overjoyed to see that you haven't redecorated." She brushed her fingers along the back of the sofa as she walked beside it. "It is such a lovely room."

"Yes, this room is quite lovely, as is the rest of the house," LaVet commented.

"Well... If I had become mistress of this fine house there are a few things I would have updated. The entrance hall is in terrible need of new wallpaper and I would look into having a few of the sofas reupholstered so they don't look so... worn." The comment was punctuated by a sweet smile that was clearly forced.

"Thank you for the kind suggestions, however, I have no wish to refurbish any of the spaces at the moment."

"I suppose that is your privilege." Lady Abney took her seat once again. "Will the master of the house be joining us?"

"He is on business with his steward. I will gladly inform him of your visit."

"I have heard the most amazing, and clearly impossible stories. I had hoped he would be able to put my mind at ease, regarding them."

Before she could explain further, the door to the sitting room opened and Lady Maren entered.

Lady Abney was on her feet again in an instant and greeted Lady Maren so warmly and with what seemed like genuine affection that LaVet felt as though she had been talking to an entirely whole other person.

Taking both of Lady Maren's hands in hers, Lady Abney leaned in and kissed both her cheeks. "How well you look, Lady Maren! There is nothing more that could make this visit more agreeable than adding your company to our conversation."

"Thank you for the compliment Lady Abney-- and how do you like my new granddaughter?" Lady Maren asked, as she reached for LaVet's hand, and took the empty chair next to her.

"She is singular." Lady Abney forced another sweet smile.

"It is kind of you to come calling," Lady Maren commented.

"Oh of course, I had to meet Kenric's new bride after hearing such... stories about her."

LaVet felt herself bristle at the casual and all too familiar use of her husband's Christian name.

"Stories?" she asked.

Lady Abney waved a hand and laughed, "Yes, from what I heard I was half expecting a wild woman. I mean, you never do really know what you're getting in these arranged marriages do you? And of course, out of concern for such dear old friends as the Leighton family, I made it a priority to meet her right away, so I could put any falsehoods to rest."

"How... kind?" LaVet cocked her head to one side and waited for Lady Abney's further explanation.

"Well, Mrs. Long came first, early this very morning, to welcome me home. She sang your praises. Of course, she has never had any ill to say of anyone," Lady Abney stated, as though Mrs. Long's opinion of others had no bearing to anyone of consequence. "Then I was informed that the new mistress of Leighton Manor was seen out hunting with a large party of men. Not riding along during a fox hunt, as is considered by those in society to be an accepted activity for genteel women, but with gun in hand...shooting pheasant!" Lady Abney said, sounding very shocked.

"I was taken aback once more when my own father, said that he had seen her racing on a great white beast of an animal-- astride, like a man! I said it could not be true. Kenric would surely temper such behavior and restrain his wife from taking part in activities that would cast her in... an unfavorable light," Lady Abney finished in a softer tone, as if she was worried that LaVet's reputation was already tarnished beyond that which could possibly be recovered.

Lady Maren murmured, "So, out of concern, you came to... make sure these reports were untrue?"

"Yes. As you know, Lady Maren, I detest gossip and cannot rest until I am able to put a stop to these rumors... if they are indeed rumors?" Her eyebrows lifted in question.

"I hate to disappoint you, Lady Abney, but it is all truth." After being talked about as if she was not present in the room, LaVet addressed her guest, drawing her attention from Lady Maren to herself. "I do enjoy a good run on my horse, and was invited to join the hunting party by my husband, and if Kenric is not troubled by my participation in these activities then I do not see why it should be any concern those so unconnected to us." LaVet knew she was being rude, yet, was unable to stop the flow of words as they rushed out.

"Well, I have been mistaken. Pardon my interference in the matter. It was kindly meant and I have full faith in such an old friend as Kenric that he must know his own mind on the subject of his wife's *acceptable* activities."

"Lady Abney, from one old friend to another, as you have pointed out, let me reassure you that there is nothing in LaVet's character that would cause shame to any in this household. You can say to those who have nothing better to do than partake in idle gossip, with my regards."

LaVet smiled at Lady Maren with new respect.

***

"Lord Leighton, we were not expecting you back so early," Collingwood said, as he met Kenric at the door.

"The property line dispute did not take as long to resolve as was first expected." Kenric removed his riding gloves and handed them to Collingwood. "I noticed a carriage out front. Who has come to call?"

"Lady Abney has come to 'inspect' your bride," Collingwood said, with lightly veiled disdain.

"Lady Abney, you say." Kenric eyed the closed sitting room door with trepidation.

"Yes sir."

Kenric looked from the closed door just down the hall to Collingwood. "How do you think it's faring?"

Collingwood gave the slightest hint of a smile. "Your wife has yet to rout the lady, so I would venture to guess... as well as possible."

"I would hate to interrupt their discussion. Perhaps it would be best if I waited for a report of Lady Abney's visit." Kenric knew it was the coward's way out.

"I think that a wise decision."

"Right then. I'll be in my study," Kenric said, then thought to add. "Collingwood, please inform my wife of my return-- *after* Lady Abney has vacated the manor."

Collingwood merely nodded his understanding.

***

It was early evening when LaVet learned that Kenric had returned and was expecting her in his study.

"What did you think of Lady Emmaleen Abney?" Kenric asked, closing the book he had been reading as LaVet strode into his study.

"I do not think she and I will be friends," LaVet said as she sank onto the settee near him.

Kenric only lifted one eyebrow as LaVet continued, "I had the feeling during our conversation that she fancied herself as the future mistress of this house."

"Emmaleen Abney fancies herself a great many things, most of which are not true," he observed with a wicked grin. "Is that your reason for not wishing to be friends with her? That she is envious of you?"

"Envious?"

"Yes, for you are where she aspires to be." LaVet looked over at him. The book was still resting between his hands, as if at any moment he would return to reading and dismiss her.

"I think she is displeased with the circumstances and felt entitled to insult our home as well as myself. I do not think she and I will be friendly, because Lady Abney does not wish to be. I have undoubtedly wronged her by becoming your wife."

"I am the better for it, and can't say that I am at all saddened by her discontent." With that statement the book reopened and Kenric disappeared behind it, as LaVet knew he would. Alone with his words she mulled them over for a minute then dared to interrupt his reading once more.

"I find you very puzzling indeed, Lord Leighton. There are times when I cannot make you out at all." The book lowered, but lay open in his lap.

"How so?"

"Much of the time I feel as though I misunderstand your meaning. Often you sound as if you insult me and yet, offering a compliment in the same breath. Do you mean to say, you are better off with my not being friends with our closest neighbor out of the inconvenience it may cause you if she liked me?"

"I never feared that Emmaleen would desire your friendship." Feeling a rush of anger LaVet stood and looked at him in the firelight.

"Clearly you and Lady Abney are of one mind. She is most convinced that I am shaming your good name by my every action. And, I know I must displease you greatly... there is little hope for change there, I am afraid. I have always been a disappointment to those who had expectations of me.

"Yet, I had hoped to have one kindred soul in this new place, where I find myself alone so much of the time. It was my dearest wish that Lady Abney would not find my company as utterly abhorrent as... *others* seem to, and that we could form an attachment."

Swallowing hard and pressing forward with the last vestiges of her courage, LaVet rushed on. "It was clear from the moment she arrived I was beneath her, and she made a point of expressing her distaste for me as well as her incredulity that you would lower your standards so far as to consent to marry *me*. I suppose I should not be astonished to find that you think along those same lines." Turning on her heel, skirts whirling around her ankles, LaVet made to flee from the library.

Kenric stopped her with one hand gripping her wrist, arresting her escape from his presence. The book clattered forgotten to the carpet under his feet.

"I was told of your temper," he laughed from close behind her. "After so lengthy a marriage I felt sure there must have been an exaggeration, but I realize now what the warnings were for."

LaVet had said her peace and set her chin firmly as he placed his hands on her shoulders and turned her to face him.

"You are correct, you did indeed misunderstand my meaning. I am sorry that Lady Abney is so blind and selfish. She is a very accomplished woman with many qualities that are prized in certain circles. Her physical beauty is a topic of many conversations." LaVet felt her anger turn to disappointment as Kenric spoke. "Yet, I am glad you are not she. I am most fortunate because *you* are my wife and she is not."

Astonished with disbelief, LaVet looked up at her husband. His eyes darkened as they held hers for a moment before Kenric went on, "She will never have your spirit or your temperament, plainly… and is truly missing out on the opportunity for a great friendship"

She wasn't able to suppress a smile at this and watched the edges of his eyes crinkling as his own smile reached them.

"I am truly sorry that you and Grandmother had to sit through her visit; yet, I cannot say I am sorry my homecoming was delayed until after she had arrived. I have had my fill of Lady Abney for a lifetime." LaVet had never heard Kenric say anything less than favorable about anyone before. His hold on her tightened as he continued.

"Indeed, you do not know your own merits. The boundless joy you have for life and your love of everything good in it has lifted the spirits of my grandmother. Your charity to the farmers and townspeople has endeared you to them as nothing could.

"You have the kindest heart I have ever known, and with it you bring harmony to my home… to those that live and work here. I have been a witness to your generosity and its effects countless times in the past weeks. And I myself have been the recipient of your counsel; something I am deeply grateful for. You are precisely everything I wished for in a wife."

Kenric added the last in a low voice, and as it left his lips he seemed as surprised with himself for saying it as LaVet was at hearing the sentiment. The room now seemed peculiarly warm as she stood under Kenric's unrelenting gaze, and she was keenly aware that his hands still rested on her shoulders.

After several painful heartbeats LaVet was able to find her voice. "I am?"

She wanted to ask more, to press him and then express all those emotions that she had been struggling with, but nothing more would come to her lips.

One of Kenric's hands left her shoulder and his fingers brushed her cheek before returning to its former place at her shoulder. "There are few that could hold a candle to you, my dear... sweet... wife, and none at all in my eyes."

Was that a declaration? LaVet wondered, as she searched for the answer in his stormy grey eyes. There *was* something burning in their depths that made her insides twist in a painfully pleasant way.

"I have become very happy in our home," she breathed.

Kenric searched her face and for a fleeting moment she wondered if he would kiss her. Abruptly, he seemed to realize how closely he was standing to her, how he was still clasping her shoulders and he immediately stepped back, dropping his hands from her.

"I am glad to hear it. You and I have become... good friends, and I would be tremendously troubled if you were at all unhappy." He was no longer looking at her, but into the fire.

LaVet forced in a breath, pulling it past the crushing feeling that was welling up inside her chest. He was reminding her that all their relationship could ever-- would ever be-- was nothing more than a friendly exchange between two unceasingly indifferent people. Remembering the brief moment when it seemed he might kiss her made her now feel foolish.

"Grandmother, I thought you had retired for the evening," Kenric said, as Lady Maren entered the room and came close to take a chair near where the two of them stood.

"No, I was too worked up by our visit with Lady Abney, and I was concerned about you, my dear." She reached out a hand toward LaVet, who took it and was drawn next to her side. LaVet went down on her knees in front of the chair that offered a respite to Lady Maren, and smiled up at the woman who was so dear to her.

"That horrid woman. I am glad to be rid of her," Lady Maren said in a huff, then with kind eyes asked, "You didn't let that silly woman's words hurt you, did you?"

"I was upset," LaVet answered truthfully, then felt a flush of heat race into her cheeks as the words exchanged only moments before came back to her mind. "Your grandson was able to talk some sense back into me, and I will never allow Lady Abney's words to affect me again." *Or my own feelings rush to judgment*, she thought to herself, stealing a glance at Kenric.

With a warm smile Lady Maren looked up at Kenric. "That's my boy." Then she patted LaVet's hand affectionately. "You do look very flushed, dear, I think rest will do us both a world of good, and by tomorrow, this night will be nothing more than a mildly unpleasant memory."

LaVet merely nodded, even though her heart was not totally in agreement.

Lady Maren extracted herself from the chair with some help, then took LaVet's arm.

"Will you escort me to my chambers? I am afraid I am too tired to manage wretched stairs on my own."

"Of course," LaVet smiled and the two women started toward the door. She glanced back at Kenric, to gauge his thoughts at the interruption of their near kiss, but he was no longer by them in the library fire. Rather he had taken his grandmother's free arm and was walking with them.

LaVet felt a rush of respect for him, for a man so diligent and thoughtful toward his aging grandmother. His treatment of Lady Maren always impressed her as the finest example of a gentleman's manners.

After a long trek to Lady Maren's chambers where her maid awaited her, LaVet found herself alone once more with Kenric. Their footfalls were the only sound between them as he walked with her down the hall in the direction of her own rooms.

Something intangible had changed and its heaviness hung in the air around her, pressing forcibly downward until it became difficult for her to draw breath.

"Would you like to join me for a ride tomorrow morning?" Kenric asked, breaking the silence.

"I would, very much. Thank you," she replied, as they reached her door and paused; each turning toward the other but averting their eyes.

"LaVet,"

"Yes, my Lord?"

"Are you truly happy here, as you said before?" There was such concern in his tone that it tore her heart to hear it.

Lifting her gaze she looked up at him and witnessed again the storm raging in the grey depths of his eyes; its power barely contained.

Not wishing him to see her distressed, she lied, "I can not remember a time when I have been more content."

~ Chapter Nine ~

LaVet was in the study working diligently on a letter to her father while Lady Maren answered a few of her own, when Kenric entered the study.

"I will be gone today. Collingwood and I have been called away to attend to some estate business, I'm afraid," Kenric announced. "May I do anything for either of you before we leave?"

"Shall we keep supper for you?" Lady Maren asked.

Kenric gave LaVet a look that made something flutter in the pit of her stomach. "I hope return this evening. If I am not home in time, please dine without me."

Lady Maren stood slowly. "I must speak with cook about the menu." Kenric moved to place a brief kiss on her cheek before she left, then he turned to LaVet.

"What will you do today?" he asked.

"Mrs. Long and I are to visit the sick and widowed this morning in Tredan, so I will be kept out of trouble for the time being," she teased.

Kenric nodded then seemed to hesitate a moment.

"Is there something more you would like me to do?" she asked, when he seemed unable to speak his thoughts.

He shook his head then, reaching for her hand placed a kiss to it and left her wondering about had been left unsaid.

***

Kenric sighed heavily as he dismounted, and with a weary Collingwood at his side trudged toward the manor; sleep hanging heavily over them both.

"Get some rest, Collingwood. Tomorrow also looks to be a very long day."
Kenric slapped the older man on the shoulder just as a mousy young girl rushed toward
the two of them.

"Sir, this was delivered for you today. I was told it was a matter of great
urgency," the little household maid stammered, as she thrust a small parcel toward
Kenric.

"Thank you." He accepted it and took his leave, heading towards his study. The
room was dark, with just the faintest glow cast from the embers of an unattended fire.
Rolling his sore shoulders and loosening the cravat around his neck, Kenric set to work
opening the parcel. He looked aghast at the portrait that unrolled into his hand.

Emmaleen's captivating smile and the brightness of her eyes had been captured
by the artist with startling accuracy in the miniature painting. Her feminine scrawl
scribbled across a small peace of parchment tied to the portrait.

My Dearest,

I looked for love and I found you. Now that we have been separated I have
sent a token of my affection to serve as a reminder that the deepest wishes of my
heart have remained unchanged.

Forever yours,

Emmaleen

Anger flared inside him. Taking both the letter and portrait he tossed them
together into the fire. Watching for several minutes as the heat caught hold and in turn
reduced them to ash; a slight rustle behind him made Kenric tense and turn sharply
toward the set of high backed chairs facing the fire. Curled up in one of them was LaVet.

Her dark head lolled to one side and her arms were folded tightly over her middle to conserve warmth.

For several seconds Kenric just stood and stared at her in wonder. Here, so close that he could smell the scent of her, was the woman who had captivated him completely. With such feelings how was it possible to contemplate Lady Abney's overt advances? She had not wanted him when Kenric had been unattached and now he'd received three notes in one week. The boldness with which she so erroneously acted left a vile taste in his mouth.

LaVet shivered slightly in her sleep, the action bringing Kenric back to his wits. Taking up a warm quilt he gently laid it across her lap. Her shivering calmed, and feeling the lateness of the hour, Kenric fell back into his own chair.

***

The fire died down to warm glowing embers and the night's chill crept in and filled the space, awakening LaVet.

A warm blanket had been draped across her lap. "I didn't mean to disturb you." She startled and looked at the chair across from her. Where Kenric sat watching her.

"I did not mean to fall asleep," she said, pulling the covering closer around her. "Have you just returned?" she asked, pressing the back of her hand tightly to her lips in an attempt to stifle a yawn.

"I have been home for a short while," Kenric sighed, looking weary.

Sitting forward, LaVet asked with concern, "Are you all right?"

"I do not wish to plague you with my troubles." His attempt to smile away her worries failed.

"I am your wife, Kenric; your troubles are mine as well." In the dim light she could see him studying her face intently.

Kenric stood and moved to the hearth. One arm rested on the mantel, his head against it, eyes fixed on the dying embers. LaVet slipped the blanket from her lap and laid it over the arm of her chair. Rising from it she walked to stand near him.

She hesitated a few moments, then placed a hand tentatively on his arm. The contact was the first voluntary touch she had shared with Kenric. All previous contact had been out of expectation, duty or accidental.

Not once had those brief touches stirred something inside her as it did now, and when his hand moved to cover hers, the air in her lungs rushed out. LaVet dared not to move, to draw another breath, or the spell would be broken.

Without lifting her eyes from the image of his hand over hers she could tell his eyes were once again on her. It was uncanny how she always knew beyond a doubt when his gaze turned in her direction.

"Tomorrow…we can talk tomorrow. It is late," Kenric said finally. Reluctantly nodding her agreement LaVet moved to take her leave and retire. As her hand slipped from his arm Kenric's fingers closed around hers and she was pulled back toward him. She looked up at him in surprise.

"I'm sorry LaVet, I do not mean to sound cross. It has been a very long day. I am worn."

"I understand," she whispered, as her heart beat loudly.

"Do not think that I mean to dismiss your concern, or that I do not appreciate your waiting for my return." His thumb ran slow circles over the back of her hand.

"I did not wait as faithfully as I should, I'm afraid. I didn't realize how tired I was after returning home myself."

"I did not think to ask how your day went. I apologize." He was still tightly holding her hand.

"Tomorrow... we can talk tomorrow." She smiled at him. "Now you must rest."

***

Kenric still looked worn the next morning when he met LaVet and his grandmother for breakfast. He hadn't even taken a bite when the door flew open and Collingwood rushed in, breathless. "Excuse my intrusion, my Lord."

"What is it Collingwood?" Kenric stood abruptly.

Collingwood looked from Kenric to LaVet with worried eyes. "You have...someone here to see you."

Kenric seemed to understand something that was unperceived by LaVet, and he promptly stood and left the room. LaVet looked at Lady Maren.

"Should I be worried?" she asked.

"No one should worry. It is a useless pastime and *you* are not useless." Lady Maren chastised her.

"I feel at a loss--" Whatever LaVet was about to say was swept aside as Lady Maren cut her off with a wave of her hand.

"I learned very early in my own marriage that part of my husband's responsibilities would take him away from me. They would weigh on his mind both night and day at times. I learned to share him with all those he offered protection to; all those who lived and worked on his land. Your marriage will be divided between the demands of his title and yourself." Maren paused for a moment.

"Kenric will always be called upon to settle disputes, to satisfy and appease where he can and to pass judgment when needed. Some wives choose not to become involved. They do not wish to become their husband's partners, or to be bothered by the lives of others. And then there are wives like you, my dear." Maren stood and moved slowly to stand next by LaVet's chair, resting a hand briefly on her shoulder.

With that, she too left the room and LaVet found herself alone, pondering what she had just been told. It did not take long for her to make up her mind, and with a prayer for strength in her heart she made her way down to the entrance hall, looking for any sign of her husband.

The sound of sobbing turned her footsteps and guided her toward the smaller of the sitting rooms. Pushing the doors open her eyes fell on a young woman who was excessively distressed and crying hard into her hands.

LaVet took in the girl's appearance; she was dressed in a gown that once may have been very fine, but now was caked with dirt and torn in a few places. Her hair looked as if it had been carefully pinned into place but some mishap had shaken many of the chocolate locks free.

"Please don't cry," she said, and watched the girl startle to find she was no longer alone. "I'm sorry, I did not mean to frighten you," LaVet said softly, and stepped closer.

"My Lady!" The girl shot from her seat and, quickly wiping her eyes, gave a curtsy.

"No, none of that. Please sit back down." LaVet took her by the hands and guided her back down, taking a seat herself. "Is there anything I can do to help you?"

She shook her head, the blue eyes red-rimmed. "No, there is nothing that can be done." The sound of despair was clear in her tone.

"What is your name?" LaVet asked.

"Caroline Ludlow."

"Hello Caroline. My name is LaVet." She took out her handkerchief and handed it to Caroline. "Do dry your eyes."

"Thank you."

"Isn't there anything I can do?" LaVet asked.

"I'm afraid there is nothing that can be done," Caroline said, her eyes downcast.

LaVet didn't press further, but whatever was weighing the child seemed too heavy not to come spilling out into the open, and she hesitantly began to pour her heart out. As her story unfolded LaVet felt the heat rising in her blood with each passing second.

Several minutes later Kenric, Collingwood and a man LaVet could only assume was Caroline's father entered the room. Kenric looked in surprise from Caroline to LaVet then his features darkened.

"Collingwood, could you see to Mr. and Miss Ludlow's needs for me. I will return shortly."

LaVet knew instinctively that she was meant to follow Kenric from the room. She gave Caroline's hand a squeeze of reassurance then left, shadowing the footfalls of her husband.

Kenric opened the door to the library and held it for her to pass through. Once she entered it closed behind her-- hard.

She faced Kenric and before he was able to open his mouth she rushed to speak. "You aren't going to send that poor girl home to be bartered away in marriage, are you?"

"LaVet, the situation is more complicated than you know," Kenric said, rubbing the back of his neck with one hand.

"She is in love with him, this young man, Peter Decker, and he is in love with her. Despite the disapproval of their fathers over the difference in fortune, there is nothing holding them back from marrying. What more is there to know?"

A rush of anger swept through him and Kenric stepped closer to her. "Caroline Ludlow was promised to someone else. Did she tell you that? Did she tell you that she and Peter ran off together the night before last to elope, and that if she hadn't been found she would have been ruined by him?

"Any prospects of a good marriage would have been lost. If this man that she loves was truly a man of honor he would never have tried to run off with her. Defying her father and damaging her reputation-- these are not the acts of love. It was lust and selfishness." Kenric had not stopped to allow her to comment but rushed forward, frustration and anger lacing his words.

He watched as LaVet lifted her jaw in defiance. "Have you, yourself spoken to Caroline? Or is all your information based on your conversations with her father?" She pressed.

"I've talked with both Mr. Ludlow and the senior Mr. Decker," he said, feeling suddenly very fatigued.

"What did Peter's father say?"

"LaVet, I promise we will make time to discuss this later. For now, please just stay here."

"No," she protested. "I need you to listen to me… please."

"The matter is no longer under discussion," Kenric snapped, regretting it instantly. "I am sorry, I do not mean to speak so harshly to you," He said in softer tones, stepping to the door. "I must return."

"What did Peter's father say?" she pursued, again and Kenric relented when it was clear that LaVet wasn't about to recede.

"He said his son is indeed in love with Miss Ludlow. He had every intention of asking for her hand despite the disapproval from both families, and has no idea of his son's current whereabouts."

"The disapproval is based on Peter's lack of fortune?"

"She is of… a different class… higher and used to a very different way of life. Mr. Ludlow believes that his daughter would only find heartache in a match with such low connections as the Deckers.

"After their discussion, Peter went missing. Later I received word from Mr. Ludlow that his daughter was gone as well and…a magistrate was needed before blood was shed. Now I must return and see if this situation can be remedied to a degree."

"Have *you* thought to talk to Caroline? Ask *her* why she was found alone, and where she thinks Peter might be. She could certainly shed some light on the events of the last two days. After all if they meant to elope, why separate? Not to mention asking her opinion on her father's choice in a husband."

"Do not let your own feelings about arranged marriages cloud your better judgment. It is a good match for her," Kenric argued, and ran a hand through his hair in frustration.

LaVet looked angrily at him. "How dare you! It is low to try and make this about our situation. I thought you were a better man than that. I had thought you were different; that you valued the opinions of others-- or is that an exclusive privilege only bestowed to men—or of those who would never present opposing views to your own? Do you dismiss Caroline because she is a woman?" As the accusation left her lips Kenric found himself working hard to remain calm. He clenched his jaw tightly while waiting for the anger to subside.

"I'm sorry," LaVet whispered, after a few moments of painful silence. She stared at him intently while taking a few steadying breaths.

"Kenric... I did not mean to say such things. You have always considered my opinion before and never made me feel as though it... didn't matter to you." Kenric noted the tears that now brimmed her eyes. "Please... do not be angry with me."

"There are times when you make it very hard not to be." Kenric reached out and brushed a tear aside that had escaped her rapid blinking. Unable to stop the impulse he then gathered her into his arms, her cheek pressed to his chest. LaVet made no move to extricate herself, and for the briefest span of time Kenric allowed himself to hold her, before stepping back and looking into her eyes.

"I am not angry. Although I don't altogether approve of your methods at times, you are right in this instant. In order to be a fair judge I need all possible information," he said, then sighing, went on. "We've left them too long." Kenric opened the door and gestured for LaVet to once again follow him.

Caroline was still crying softly. Her father, looking angry, paced the floor behind her chair. Kenric proceeded to take a seat near Caroline and looked at the young woman.

"Miss Ludlow, I have talked to both your father and Mr. Decker. Now, would you please tell me what happened?"

"I've told you already! Now I want you to do something. I demand justice for the dishonor forced onto my family, and assurances that the marriage arranged for my daughter will not be compromised!" Mr. Ludlow bellowed.

Kenric shot the man a withering look, then looked back to his daughter. "Please, allow her to speak."

The older man grunted in disapproval. "There is nothing she would tell you that would be of import," her father snapped.

"Mr. Ludlow, if you would like my help, I require your silence at this moment," Kenric said so forcefully there was no room for further argument. He once again turned his attention to Caroline.

She gulped and dried her eyes with the handkerchief LaVet had given her. "Lord Leighton, I am sure many of the details of what happened two days ago have been left unsaid. My father forbade me to see Peter and told me of the arranged marriage. I, in turn, acted rashly and fled my father's house to find Peter."

"To run away with him?" Kenric asked.

"I went to beg him to run away with me to Scotland and elope, yes. But Peter told me there was no honor in elopement and that he would never take me to wife in such a manner. He said he was determined to change both our father's minds and have their blessings on our union."

"How did he plan on doing that?" Kenric pressed.

"He wouldn't tell me. He sent me home... I had no idea he was missing as well until I was found by Mr. Collingwood."

"If you were not with Peter these last two days, where have you been?"

"I... I hid." Kenric raised an eyebrow at her statement and waited for her to explain. "I was frightened and had nowhere to go. So, I hid. Spending the night in the barn, I remained there until I was too hungry to stay. That's when I stumbled across Mr. Collingwood's path."

"So, you and Peter did not run away together after all." Kenric sat back and rubbed his chin then looked at her father. "Mr. Ludlow you led me to believe something very different. Did you truly turn your daughter out of your home?"

"How I choose to deal with my daughter is my concern."

Kenric stood, rising to his full height. "Mr. Ludlow, when you came to ask for my help in finding your daughter and defamed the character of two innocent young people you made it my concern."

Kenric turned to LaVet. "Would you take Miss Ludlow in to breakfast? I think her father, Mr. Decker and I have some things to discuss."

***

LaVet ate dinner alone for the fifth day in a row. Lady Maren had been taken ill and kept to her room. Kenric left with Peter's father to search him out and Caroline had been shipped off for an extended stay with her Aunt.

Throwing herself into the various distractions of everyday life helped to pass the time, doing more charity work with Mrs. Long, going on rides, and even welcoming a visit from Lady Abney, who only wanted to talk about her displeasure with everything on God's green earth and then left without hearing a word from LaVet. She wasn't able to remember a time when she had felt more alone.

"Do I need to speak with cook about the quality of your food?" LaVet jumped at the sound of Kenric's voice.

"No, the food is fine." She had been so lost in thought that his entrance had gone unnoticed.

"Then why haven't you touched it?" He slid into the chair across from her at the dining table.

She looked down at her plate and realized he was correct. She had moved a few items around but hadn't eaten anything. "I suppose I am not very hungry."

Kenric leaned forward and looked closely at her, "If you are not inclined to finish your dinner would you consider taking a turn with me in the gardens?"

"Of course." LaVet pushed her chair back and, taking his arm, they walked out to the warmth of the garden and the last vestiges of the day.

They walked for several minutes before Kenric cleared his throat. "Have you been well in my absence?"

"I have been fully occupied," she answered simply, then pressed forward with what she really wanted to discuss. "Were you able to find Peter?"

"His father and I did locate him." Kenric sighed, "After Peter was dismissed from Mr. Ludlow's home he did some thinking about his future. He has decided that his best avenue is to make his own way; proving to himself more than anyone, that he could make more of himself than what he was born to."

"How does he plan to do that?" she pressed.

"Peter has joined the Royal Navy. His father is sad to have lost his help on the farm, but is proud of his decision all the same."

"What do you think will happen to them? Caroline and Peter?"

"LaVet, you were right to... remind me, that to be a fair magistrate I needed to hear all sides; to take into consideration every aspect of the given situation. However, not every result is the one hoped for. We cannot presume to interfere beyond what is asked, no matter how our emotions may try to sway us.

"In the future I will be called upon to give counsel over innumerable misunderstandings or infractions. I hope that those things will not negatively affect *our* relationship. We are partners in this life, LaVet; we must learn to stand together and always be cautious of imposing our values on others."

"I apologize for my interference; it was not meant to cause harm in anyway," she said in a soft voice.

Kenric bent his head low over his chest and closed his eyes for a moment before responding, "I know of a man and woman who married for love. It is not a bad idea in principle, and for many the chance to truly follow your heart leads to happiness in this life. There are those that live poor and happy, while others with wealth are miserable.

"This particular couple was in much the same circumstances as Peter and Caroline, although it was the young man who was blessed with lands and riches while the lady was poor, yet beautiful. His family opposed the match and insisted he marry another. When he refused and ran off with the woman who is now his wife, he was cut off from the larger part of his inheritance and lost a great deal of wealth."

Kenric paused as they passed the gardener who was cleaning up trimmings and undergrowth from around a freshly cut hedge.

"He was left with his title, a house in London and nothing more. At first, they lived in economy and seemed very happy. As time passed and children were added their marriage took a turn. You see, this lady, she was not all that she appeared. She had wanted to marry for comfort, wealth, and status; only some of which he was able to supply.

"She no longer loved him or the idea of their life together and sought companionship elsewhere. Her unfaithfulness was masked well for many years as their marriage continued to decline. But all lies tend to rise to the surface. The husband became bitter and distrustful of any woman. Drink and constant travel became his only recourses to deal with the miserable state he now found himself in."

"Could he not seek a divorce on the grounds of her unfaithfulness?" she asked quietly.

"He could, and would be justified, but love is a peculiar thing. He is still in love with the woman he married. Not the person she chose to become, but with the hope that that person will reemerge."

"What a dreadfully miserable way to live."

"I've known others who married for very different reasons; people who were not in love but grew to have a strong mutual respect for one another. That respect can often be a precursor to deeper, richer feelings as the relationship grows." Kenric's voice was low and full as he added the last sentence. LaVet wasn't able to stop herself from gazing up at him for a stolen moment.

Long after she had looked back down she could feel his eyes still on her.

"I wished to illustrate that happiness in one's marriage is completely based on one's own choice to be so, and not particularly based on the circumstances that led to the union. I cannot say whether Peter and Caroline will one day marry, but her reputation is unblemished, and that alone is a blessing."

Again they fell into silence and walked for several minutes until she was able to find her voice once more.

"Kenric, I must beg your forgiveness. I acted impulsively—selfishly, and you were right to censure me for… well, for letting my own views on marriage cloud my better judgment, as you put it." LaVet found it hard to admit her feelings on the subject, especially to Kenric, but she forced herself to continue.

"I should never have allowed my emotions to gain the better of me. It is a defect of my person that runs too deeply. It is important for Caroline to have her reputation untarnished. For a woman, it is one of the only things of real value she has to offer a prospective husband and she acted rashly… thoughtlessly. I too am guilty of that."

LaVet slipped her hand from his arm, "I must also apologize for my outburst. You were correct in your conviction that I was indeed allowing my personal feelings about arranged marriages influence my reaction to Caroline's story. I am so ashamed of how I behaved."

"I had thought you were happy here; content with your life and position. Have you really been so miserable and I so blind to have not noticed?" Kenric asked from a few steps to her left.

LaVet spun around to face him. "No, I am very content."

"Then please, enlighten me as to why you have such a displeasing view of arranged marriages?"

Unable to look at him as she answered, LaVet turned from his storm grey eyes. "I count myself among the very blessed. You are a good man… a good husband. I have not been abused or treated poorly. Over the past months of our marriage I have grown accustomed to… to our arrangement. However, not all are so fortunate. It is those cases which I use as a reference for my personal distaste for the practice."

"Do you still hold resentment toward your father for arranging our union?"

"I suppose I could have… made things more difficult for him. Protested the idea more fervently than I did. Even run away if I had been so inclined. But I do not see myself in the same position as Peter and Caroline," she answered.

"Knowing your temper as I now do and your propensity for wishing to always be in the right, I wonder that you didn't fight your father at the prospect." Kenric's voice held a hint of humor to it.

"I was made fully aware of what our marriage would accomplish. I was not forgoing anything, such as the love of another, and our marriage was very advantageous for both parties." As the words were uttered an idea came to her that was so unpleasant it brought a bitter taste to her mouth to think it. "And you? What did you have to give up?"

Kenric didn't answer right away, and the longer he remained silent the harder it was for LaVet to keep her composure.

"I thought myself very much in love once," he relented. LaVet glanced up at him from the corner of her eye; he was no longer looking down at her but out toward the setting sun.

The idea that Kenric, a man eight years her senior; strong, handsome, intelligent and independently wealthy, would have never caught the eye of another woman seemed in the realm of absurdity. Yet to hear that he had once loved forced her insides to turn in a painful way, making her wish he would not elaborate further.

"I am glad to have been wrong," Kenric offered nothing further and LaVet breathed deeply in relief.

It wasn't so much the idea that he had once wished to marry another, as the thought that he might still be pining away for her-- or even more dreadful,-- might have married LaVet to insure peace while keeping this other women as his mistress. LaVet shocked herself with the idea and shook her head to displace it.

"I do believe there is a slight chill in the air tonight," Kenric observed, after a time.

"Yes, winter will soon be upon us," LaVet agreed as their footsteps led them back toward the house. The sun was setting and cast brilliant colors of gold and red on the wisps of clouds that hung low over the distant treetops.

~ Chapter Ten ~

"I was told I might find you here." LaVet looked up from her book as Kenric approached her. "It seems an odd place to read a book."

LaVet glanced at her surroundings and smiled, "This is my favorite place on the grounds." She sat under a tall willow; its branches dancing in the late summer breeze. From her vantage point she had a sweeping view of the large manor house and perfectly manicured gardens, and her tree sat right at the edge of the lawn on the verge of the woods.

"May I sit with you?" he asked, then without waiting her answer took a seat near her in the warm grass.

"I didn't think we were expecting you home today," she said, trying to sound as uninterested as possible.

"I was able to arrange things faster than I had expected."

"You have been very secretive of late; what is this business that has kept you so occupied?" she pressed.

"I'll gladly tell you if you offer up some information of your own," he said.

She cocked her head to one side, "What would you like to know?"

"Why are you reading a book on botany?" Kenric asked, and slipped the book out from under her fingertips to flip it open.

"I was studying medicinal plants that might be used to help your grandmother… perhaps with a tea or poultice. She seems to be feeling worse these last few weeks, spending more and more time resting in her room." LaVet trailed off when she noticed the look on Kenric's face.

"Do you disapprove?"

"No." Kenric caught her gaze and the soft look in his grey eyes made her breath catch. "I had thought to find you reading poetry or a novel, yet it doesn't surprise me that you would be thinking of someone else."

While he was talking his gaze never wavered from hers.

"I've answered your question; now you must return the favor," she prompted.

"You're right." The book snapped shut. "As to what has been taking up so much of my time, I've been procuring your birthday gift," Kenric said nonchalantly, and handed her back the book.

"My birthday gift?" she asked in surprise.

Kenric laughed and got to his feet, then turned and held out his hand for her to take. "What kind of a husband would I be if I forgot your birthday?"

She looked at him with curiosity then slipped her hand into his and allowed him to help her to her feet.

They started toward the house. Kenric didn't drop her hand or place it on his arm as per usual. She looked down to where her hand rested, cradled softly within the web of his fingers and wasn't able to suppress the fluttering in her stomach.

As they walked around the corner of the house two carriages were just pulling up, and the sight of the lead carriage sent a thrill through her as she instantly recognized it.

"My father? You sent for my father?" She beamed looking up at Kenric as the horses came to a stop. The carriage door opened and her father stepped out then turned, reaching a hand back where a women's gloved hand slipped into his.

LaVet watched as a very elegant, finely-dressed woman with golden hair stepped from the carriage, and her heart leapt. Then she tore away from Kenric in a dead run.

"Octavia!" she called and waved. Her sister turned at the sound of her name with a grin on her face as she caught sight of LaVet. A laugh of pure joy bubbled up as she caught her sister up in an embrace, hugging LaVet unashamedly then placing a kiss to her cheek she pulled back to look at her.

"You are more beautiful than I remembered," LaVet said, touching Octavia's face.

"You are just as wild," Octavia laughed, and reached to tuck a hair back into place that had fallen across LaVet's forehead in her dash across the lawn.

"I do apologize for my daughter, Lord Leighton. I did hope that her new station would have taught her some decorum or at least restraint." The disapproving tone in her father's voice was more than familiar to her and she turned to face him with a half smile.

"I'm very glad to see you as well, father," LaVet greeted him.

"I believe there are instances in which decorum and restraint can be overlooked, and receiving loved ones is such an occasion. It is good to see you again Lord Roche and I do hope your trip was comfortable." Kenric took his hand in a firm handshake then moved to stand next to LaVet.

LaVet smiled proudly from him to her sister. "Lord Leighton, may I have the pleasure of introducing you to my most cherished sister, Lady Octavia Stillwell." Kenric placed a kiss to Octavia's hand and gave a slight bow of respect as she curtseyed.

"It's an honor to have you, Lady Stillwell."

The door of the other carriage opened and everyone turned as two small children hopped out, followed by a pleasantly plump woman holding a small bundle.

"LaVet, please come and meet your nephew and niece." Octavia took LaVet by the arm and led her over to the small, smartly dressed boy and the tiny girl with corn-silk colored curls.

"LaVet, this is Kyrus and Ninet. Children, this is your Aunt LaVet." Bending at the waist, LaVet looked both children in the eyes and saw her sister reflected in them. Falling instantly in love, she reached out and drew them both to her.

"Welcome, to Leighton Manor." LaVet said, smiling brightly. "I am so happy you have come to visit."

"Mother said it was a surprise for your birthday. Is it really your birthday?" Ninet asked, twisting a curl around her finger.

"Yes it is," LaVet confirmed.

"Will there be cake?" she asked, and tilted her head to the side looking up at LaVet.

"Of course. It would not be a proper celebration without cake," Kenric interjected with a laugh.

"Children, this is your Uncle Kenric," Octavia smiled.

Kyrus gave Kenric an appraising look. "I thought you would be old. You're not old."

"Old enough, I'm afraid," Kenric answered. "And what about you, young man? How old are you?"

Kyrus stood straighter. "I'll be six in a month."

"You are practically a man then. Your father must rely on you heavily. I do hope you will consent to advise *me* while you are here. I could use another man's opinion."

"I… yes, I could do that," Kyrus answered eagerly, and LaVet smiled as Kenric gained a second shadow.

"LaVet, Lord Leighton, this is our governess Ann and the newest member of the family, Luette." Octavia took the small bundle from Ann and uncovered the face of a sleeping infant.

"She is perfection incarnate. You must be very proud." LaVet gladly took the baby from her sister and held her close.

"She looks like you." Octavia smiled and traced a finger over the small patch of dark hair that crowned her child's head. The two sisters smiled at each other. LaVet noted the tears brimming in Octavia's eyes and reached to pull her close.

LaVet looked around for a moment, "What of your husband? Did he not accompany you?"

"Richard was unfortunately detained, but he plans on joining us as soon as business will allow."

"How long will you be staying?" LaVet pressed.

"The invitation was for three weeks, and we plan to stay for the entirety," Octavia smiled.

"Three weeks after so many years will not be long enough." Leaning her forehead to Octavia's cheek LaVet whispered, "Oh, how I have missed you."

"As I have you."

***

Kenric laughed heartily as he played ninepins with Kyrus. Ann watched Ninet try her hand at hoops as Lady Maren and LaVet's father chatted over cake and tea.

"He is falling in love with you-- if he isn't already." Octavia smiled knowingly at LaVet as she took the open seat next to her. LaVet was bouncing Luette on her knee and stopped abruptly at her sister's words.

"What?" she gasped, as Octavia laughed aloud. "What... what on earth would make you say that?"

"He is, and if not, then why would he go to all the trouble of making arrangements to bring your only sister, her three small children and governess all this way for your birthday celebration?"

"Because he is a thoughtful man and knew that it would make me happy to see you and the children," LaVet countered.

"My dear little sister." Octavia turned to look into LaVet's face and took her free hand in her own. "After all that you have told me of your relationship with Kenric, after all the sacrifices that he has made for your comfort, the concessions given, how could you be in doubt of his feelings for you? What man who wasn't hopelessly in love would do half for his wife what Lord Leighton has done for you?

"He has not taken liberties that many men would see as their right as a husband, he has been nothing but kind and attentive. He stopped extensive travel upon your request and has taken your counsel on many occasions, not to mention his complete trust in your ability to execute the duties as the mistress of this house without interference or chastisement. Then, there is the retrieval of mother's necklace." Octavia paused as she searched LaVet's face, allowing her words to set in for a moment before asking, "How do you feel about him?"

"I… I have the highest respect for him and I do enjoy his company." Octavia cut her off with a dismissive wave of her hand.

"No, I mean how do you *feel* about him? Have you really thought about your feelings?"

LaVet felt as though her voice had abandoned her as her mind spun.

Octavia took a deep breath and, seeing that LaVet wasn't going to respond, went on in a kinder tone. "I learned early in my marriage that if I wanted to be happy, the only person that could make it so was myself. If I wanted to be in a marriage full of love, I was the only one that could do anything about it. So, I did."

"How?" LaVet pressed, remembering that Kenric had said something very similar.

"I set out to learn all I could about my new family and soon I felt as if I belonged to them and that they were mine. I spent much time learning about my husband; his likes and those things he finds passion in. Day after day I found new things to love about him, and then one day I was in love." LaVet drank in her sister's words and watched the glow in her face brighten as she talked about her husband.

"You do love Lord Stillwell, don't you?" LaVet asked, in astonishment.

"Did you think I lied in my letters?" Octavia asked, surprised.

"No…you never came right out and said it but… perhaps I thought you wanted me to believe in your happiness in order to spare my own feelings."

"Why would I do that?" Octavia asked.

"I... I... the day father told you of your marriage... and the last I saw of you, you didn't seem happy." LaVet stumbled over her words trying to explain. "Miserable, in fact."

"You have held on to the images of that day when mother told you I was to be married, and it has hardened you. Life is not always black and white—it is full of colors. Wonderful, rich colors that make up the tapestry of our world, and those colors deepen and change in their vibrancy as we grow and change as well. Do not limit yourself to a world with only two tones."

"To have a partner in this life that makes you more than you could possibly be on your own is a rare blessing," she continued, and nodded toward where Kenric was laughing heartily with Kyrus. "Do not overlook it in your marriage because it was arranged."

***

LaVet dressed for bed in a daze and lay awake for hours thinking of the conversation she had shared with her sister. She had not expected to find herself in the tumult she now experienced.

Had she really doomed herself to a life of black and white? Is that why so many things no longer held the joy they once had? How selfish she had been-- how naive? What were her feelings for Kenric, or his true feelings for her? Questions, only questions rolled through her mind as restless hours passed; questions with no answers.

***

"We have been invited to a ball," Lady Maren announced over lunch. "Now that our party has grown it seems like the perfect time to accept the engagement." LaVet glanced toward her sister and husband. Lord Richard Stillwell had come to Leighton

Manor a few days before, much to the happiness of his wife and children.

LaVet had been keen to witness the reunion, and could not deny the mutual

affection displayed between husband and wife. Richard was kind and attentive, but it was

the look in his eyes each time Octavia was in view that convinced LaVet of his true

feelings for her sister. The knowledge of their mutual love brought LaVet peace

regarding her previous suppositions of their relationship.

"The invitation was extended to include our guests as well, of course" Lady

Maren added.

"A ball? How wonderful." Octavia smiled with delight.

"Whom do we have the pleasure of thanking for this invitation?" LaVet asked.

"Sir Abney."

"When is the ball to be held?" Octavia questioned, between sips of water.

"In three day's time," Lady Maren answered.

"Shall we accept?" Kenric directed the question to LaVet.

LaVet hesitated only a moment, "Yes, of course." She watched as Octavia's face

lit up. "I suppose that now an afternoon of strawberry picking won't seem nearly as

exciting," she teased her sister.

***

"You look beautiful this evening," Kenric whispered, as he took LaVet's hand

and placed it on his arm, leading her into the large brick home of Lord Abney.

He was rewarded with a rush of color rising into her cheeks, but not satisfied, he

pressed on. "I quite like your new dress; the green is a very lovely addition." Kenric thought she looked every bit a vision in a lace dress over a satin slip with a large green sash. Leaning closer, he was able to breathe in the subtle scent of the flowers pinned into her hair.

"I was also pleased to notice that you are wearing the peacock brooch. It compliments you and brings out the emerald in your eyes."

"You must stop! I may never recover from such a torrent of compliments. Especially because I can not take you seriously when you are grinning at me like that," she protested, with a laugh.

At the top of the long staircase stood Emmaleen Abney and her father, greeting their guests. When it was the Leighton party's turn to be received Lady Abney gave Kenric a bright smile that reached her eyes; something a smile rarely did with her. He was at a loss trying to remember having previously witnessed any genuine emotion from Lady Abney.

"We are overjoyed to have you," Emmaleen greeted them, then turned to her father. "I don't believe you have met Kenric's new wife, Father. May I have the pleasure of introducing you to LaVet Leighton."

"Lord Abney, it is truly a delight." The older man took LaVet's hand and pressed a kiss to it. Kenric then presented her father, sister and husband, repeating his thanks that the invitation had been extended to include his guests.

Lord Abney greeted Lady Maren and led them all inside after taking her arm. Kenric watched LaVet with interest as she took in the richly furnished and spacious rooms.

The small group was led into the ballroom which was brightly lit; doors and windows open to allow the evening air to cool the dancers. A small orchestra was set up and ready to play.

As soon as the Abneys entered the room all eyes turned toward them. Lord Abney looked to his daughter. "Well, my dear, it is time to start the ball. With whom will you stand?"

Emmaleen glanced at all those around them. "Lord Roche, would you do me the honor?" She turned to LaVet's father, who accepted gladly.

"Lady Maren, would you like to take a turn?" Lord Abney bowed low over her hand.

Lady Maren smiled in return, "Thank you, that would be refreshing." And with that, the ball had begun.

***

Crowds of people mingled along the sides of the ballroom; cups of punch and cakes in hand. After standing up with her father, brother-in-law, Lord Abney and a few new acquaintances LaVet found much of the night had passed pleasantly. The constant movement of the dancers made the ballroom uncommonly hot. LaVet felt herself becoming faint from the heat. She turned to Lady Maren and, touching her arm, excused herself for a moment.

Not wishing to go out to the gardens for fear that she would run into someone who wished to converse, she slipped quietly into the hall and then into the next room. Needing a moment alone, LaVet found herself in a study; a warm fire burning in the hearth. She leaned on the door and let out a long sigh.

The fire cast shadows on the surrounding walls and gave no reprieve to the heat. LaVet avoided its warmth and went to the windows; pushing back the heavy curtains to allow the coolness of the night wash over her as she pushed the window open further.

The curtain fell back into place, shielding her from view and blanketing her in darkness. LaVet took a few deep breaths and tried to revive herself. Her breathing was so deep she didn't hear the door opening or the sound of footfalls approaching.

"Thank you for escorting me from of the ballroom; I was finding the heat intolerable." LaVet instantly recognized the voice of Lady Emmaleen Abney and tensed. Turning in place, she pulled back the curtain enough to see into the room but not give away her position in it.

LaVet suddenly realized she was intruding into a private room as a guest in the Abney home, and feared the reaction that she might meet with if her intrusion was revealed.

"Would you like the smelling salts?" LaVet's gaze fell on Kenric. Emmaleen was relying heavily on his arm. Something akin to anger flooded LaVet's senses at the sight.

"No, I think a few minutes away from the crowds will do me a world of good," she answered in sweet tones.

LaVet knew she should make herself known and return to the ball. Revealing her intrusion on their conversation regardless of the disapproval she would face was the only proper thing to be done.

"Lady Leighton looks very well," Emmaleen said as Kenric helped her to the long sofa then stepped away from her to lean his arm on the fireplace mantel. "She clearly dressed to advantage this evening."

"Yes, LaVet looks lovely," he agreed as LaVet's resolve to step out into the room dissolved, unabashed curiosity taking over her senses.

"And are you finding that you enjoy married life as much as you anticipated?" Emmaleen pressed. There was a tone of disapproval held in her words.

"More so," he answered. LaVet studied Kenric in profile. He looked a bit uncomfortable to her; standing rigid with jaw tensed.

"Truly? I would have thought you found it to be tedious. She… well she isn't the kind of lady I expected you to marry." Emmaleen stood and covered the distance between Kenric and herself in a few easy strides, then placed a dainty hand on his shoulder. "The offer I made you before your nuptials still stands, Kenric." Her voice was low and lustful as she addressed him. LaVet bristled at Emmaleen's tone then writhed with anger as her hand slid from his shoulder, tracing the line of his arm until her fingers rested over his.

"Lady Abney, if I did not take you up on the offer when first presented, what on earth would make you believe that I would do so now?" Kenric shook off her hand and turned to face her, his eyes hard, like tempered steel.

Emmaleen laughed off the question. "You have been imprisoned up in that manor house with a *girl* for a little over six months. I expected that you would…"

"I would what?" he growled. "That I would break my marriage vows? That I would take you as a mistress?"

"Would it really be so strange? Many noblemen engage a mistress and I am not opposed to the idea." LaVet's hand flew to her mouth to cover a gasp. She watched as both of Emmaleen's hands came up to rest on Kenric's chest and she leaned closely into him.

"Do not dishonor yourself any further. I must return to the ball and my *wife*." He removed her hands from him and stepped to the side, putting space between them.

"You say this now, but there may come a time when you again crave my company," Emmaleen shot back. "You loved me once, remember?"

"Lady Abney, if I can still presume to call you Lady, I have never craved your company in the manner in which you are suggesting, and I can't see myself doing so in the future. As to my being in love with you…" Kenric paused as he shook his head. "I can honestly say I have no idea who you are, so it is impossible for feelings of that nature to have developed between us." He turned sharply and prepared to exit the room.

"It was to be me!" she screamed at his retreating back "*I* was to be the mistress of Leighton Manor, not some child! If only you had not entered into this sham of a marriage-- this disgusting arrangement only in order to provide her mad father with money and a pathetic truce-- then *I* would be by your side and you would have grown to love *me*."

Kenric stopped, his hand on the door, and turned to look back at Emmaleen, who now had tears streaming down her face. "Is that truly what you believe? Let me enlighten you." His voice had gone cold.

LaVet had never seen Kenric look so angry before and the way his eyes darkened made her shiver.

"I was married to LaVet with no dowry or money exchanging hands between myself and her father. The marriage has nothing to do with either parties finances, I am independently wealthy and will enjoy a substantial income the rest of my life. Her 'mad father' as you called him, will leave his son a great estate along with a fortune of twenty thousand pounds a year upon his death.

"Lord Roche chooses to live his life more secluded than most and in economy, it is true, but do not mistake that for foolishness or poverty. He has grown his estates' wealth ten-fold since the passing of his father. My marriage was arranged, as you say; both families having desired peace between our houses for many years and our union ensuring that."

"How contriving of you. What of love, passion, true companionship?" She wept and threw herself toward him.

"None of which you present to me in your offer," he countered, peeling her from him and setting her back on her feet.

"I would have given you everything, Kenric!" she cried. "I still can… if you let me."

"Emmaleen, stop this at once." Kenric took her by the shoulders, calling her by her Christian name and shaking her out of her hysteria. "Do not throw away your opportunity for a good marriage. I am devoted to my wife. You still have the chance to find someone devoted only to you. I am sorry I am not that man."

Emmaleen tore free from his hold and with fresh tears turned sharply from him.

"Do you really care for her?" she asked, her voice broken and hollow.

LaVet held her breath as she too waited for Kenric's answer.

"More than I ever thought possible." With that he left Emmaleen standing in the middle of the room.

LaVet watched in horror as Emmaleen clutched at her middle and let out a strangled sob.

She now felt tears of her own come unbidden to her eyes, mixed emotions churning her stomach. LaVet's emotions had gone from the fear of being discovered listening to their conversation, to anger at Emmaleen's presumption, that moved swiftly into sorrow and pity for the woman. LaVet could not imagine what events could have taken place in her life to lead her to this behavior.

For such a highborn, gentlewoman of good fortune to proposition a married man and offer to become his mistress, she must indeed have little self-respect. Then to be so concisely turned down in favor of an arranged marriage-- LaVet could only imagine the conflicting emotions now raging inside the other woman.

After several painful minutes Emmaleen drew in a few deep breaths and composed herself. LaVet watched her leave the study then, calming herself, she slipped from behind the curtains.

Replaying the conversation over in her mind two things fixed her attention. The first was how honorable Kenric had been. She had once entertained doubts in regards to his fidelity and it had plagued her. Now, to hear him refuse to engage in a relationship with Emmaleen made all those fears fly and she knew she would never have reason to doubt him again.

The second idea made her knees weak; he had said he cared for her... *more than he could have thought possible*, those had been his words and they resonated within her. Something fluttered and twisted in her stomach-- it was not an entirely unpleasant feeling as she recalled the sound of Kenric's voice as he has said it. Was Octavia correct? Was he indeed falling in love with her?

Unable to stay in the study any longer she fled from the room. As she reentered the ballroom her eyes scanned the faces, looking only for one.

The dancers laughed merrily as they promenaded, the orchestra playing a lively jig. LaVet didn't notice any of it as her eyes locked on Kenric. He was standing near a chair which Lady Maren occupied, looking out over the ballroom while she chatted with him.

It seemed impossible for him to feel her gaze from across such a distance and in such a large assembly, but Kenric turned slightly and his steely grey eyes locked on hers. LaVet felt the air rush from her lungs as a smile played on the corners of his lips. Then he was moving through the crowd toward her.

"Grandmother informed me that you weren't feeling well; are you alright?" Kenric asked with concern, upon reaching the spot in which LaVet had found herself frozen.

"I am, well, just a little overly warm," she forced out, trying hard to suppress the blush that crept into her cheeks under his discerning gaze.

"Would you like something to drink? Or, perhaps a turn outside?" he pressed.

Her mind whirled, "I... I..." LaVet shook her head slightly and wished she could regain her composure and coherence.

Kenric's brow furrowed. "You are flushed. Truly, is there nothing I can do to ensure your comfort?"

"Perhaps some fresh air would be in order," She forced out. The feeling of being pressed upon by the sheer number of bodies in the room was starting to make it difficult to draw breath.

His eyes drew hers upward and she was only able to stare at him. "I will escort you wherever you wish to go," he said, taking up her hand and placing it in his arm and leading her out to the balcony, as if he were able to read her thoughts.

"Is this better?" he asked.

"Much, thank you." She breathed in deeply the crisp late September air.

"Have you been enjoying the ball?" Kenric questioned.

"Yes."

"I have been remiss in my duties as your husband. We have not yet shared a dance. It seemed that each time I turned around you were already engaged."

LaVet wasn't able to stop a smile, "I had no idea you had a mind to perform such tedious duties as to stand up with your wife in such an assembly. Perhaps in the future you should secure the first dance if you so wish and... all those that follow," she offered, and was surprised by her own boldness and flirtatious manner.

Kenric chuckled warmly and waited for another couple taking the air to pass before he answered. "I knew your counsel in this matter would prove to hold a reasonable solution." His free hand covered hers as it lay on his arm, his lean fingers curling around her slender ones, sending a powerful shock through her.

LaVet swallowed hard, knowing Kenric was watching her intently.

"Kenric, I have something I need to confess," she said, and her steps slowed.

"Confess?"

LaVet slipped her hand from his arm and took a few uneasy steps away from him.

"You have me sufficiently worried now," he quipped from close behind her.

"I've done something shameful and so… so completely unlike me." LaVet nervously rubbed at her mother's necklace, and then turned to him.

Thinking of how best to tell him, she sighed then rushed headlong into her explanation, "While you were engaged as a partner to Lady Abney I excused myself from the ballroom. After wandering the corridors I found myself in her father's study. I don't know what led me there… the fire was still glowing, and I was overheated, so I rushed to the windows and… and was taking a moment to gather myself together when…"

"You overheard my conversation with Lady Abney." He finished for her, it was not a question.

"I'm so sorry. I may have many faults but I do not make it a habit to listen in on private exchanges, but there was no opportune moment to reveal myself without making it so much worse." The apology came out in such a rush it was only half intelligible.

Kenric laughed aloud. "And this is your shameful confession?"

LaVet wasn't sure what reaction she had expected, but his deep rumbling laugh wasn't it. "Yes, the… conversation was never meant for my ears, and it's extremely inappropriate to eavesdrop."

"I am relieved."

"How so?"

"It saves me from having to relate it to you at a later time," he answered simply.

"You would have told me, then?" she asked, after a brief hesitation of disbelief.

"I have learned that attempting to hide things from you is fruitless and often leads to more complications than are necessary." LaVet smiled ruefully at his reference to her constant interference in every aspect of his business and life at the manor.

"I'm afraid that in all previous instances referred to, you would have been lost without my counsel. I act purely out of concern," she said, laughing.

"There you are," Kenric drawled in a soft voice, stepping closer to LaVet.

"Was I lost?"

"You have been withdrawn since we received the invitation; acting a part. I've missed *my* wife. The quick tongue and wit." He took another step toward her. "Do not hide from me."

"I did not intend to," LaVet breathed, her heart pounding so loudly she was positive it would burst from her chest at any moment.

Smiling warmly at her, Kenric took her hand, placing it on his arm and once again covering it with his own. They started walking again. "I suppose you acted for your sister. She did seem very happy with the prospect of a ball. However if you were uncomfortable in accepting you should have told me."

She struggled for a minute before finding her voice. "Lady Abney has never been friendly and I wasn't sure what to expect," she answered honestly.

"Is that all?" he pressed. She knew that he was well aware of every aspect of the overheard conversation. LaVet wanted to add that she saw the way Emmaleen had looked at him; that she knew that Emmaleen was the woman he had thought himself in love with once. Yet the words would not form in her mouth.

"May I ask you a question," Without waiting for her to answer, Kenric rushed on. "I have yet to claim my dance, may I do so now?" LaVet smiled and didn't protest as he led her to the floor as the next dance started, then claimed her as his partner for each succeeding dance for the reminder of the evening.

~ Chapter Eleven ~

"I never had the chance to ask you how you liked your visit with your sister?" Kenric asked, as they reined in their horses after a brisk run.

"I was overjoyed to have them all here. I believe they had a good holiday as well," LaVet responded, as she leaned forward and patted Beauty on the neck.

"I'm glad to know they found their time here pleasant. I too enjoyed their visit."

"I haven't yet thanked you for sending for them." She drew her eyes from Beauty and looked at him. "I could not have wished for a more perfect birthday gift."

"I am glad to hear it." The storm was back in his eyes, blazing with a new intensity as he returned her gaze.

"I will miss them," LaVet said, with a touch of sadness. "The house already feels quiet without the children and it's only been a few days since their departure."

"They are delightful children," He nodded, and for some time they sat atop a hill overlooking Tredan.

"I would be honored to extend the invitation any time your sister or any of your relations are inclined to accept it. I hope they always feel welcome," Kenric added, and LaVet smiled warmly at him.

"There is no fear of them feeling unwelcome; your hospitality is indisputable. I am sure any of my relations would love to accept your invitation whenever received," she assured him.

"You need not wait on me to extend an invitation; after all, Leighton Manor is your home as well."

Again her eyes were drawn to him, "Thank you." LaVet felt a flood of appreciation toward Kenric for his thoughtfulness.

She studied him more closely, feeling as though she were truly seeing him for the first time.

LaVet had spent much of her time contemplating what his feelings for her could be after Octavia had planted the idea in her mind. However, she had not spent time considering what her own were for him.

Now, there was no denying that over time her feelings had grown to encompass respect, admiration, friendship and yes, attraction-- yet she sensed something deeper as well; something she had never felt before for anyone. Could it be love?

"LaVet, did you hear me?"

She shook her head and forced her eyes to focus. "I apologize; my mind was elsewhere. What did you say?"

"I told you I will be leaving this afternoon. I have some business that requires attending. Is there anything you need before I prepare to leave?"

"I cannot think of anything. Will you be gone long?"

Kenric searched her face as he answered, "No, I will return this evening."

"Well then, I suppose our morning ride has come to an end. Shall we return home?" she asked, and gathered the reins more tightly in her hand.

Kenric nodded and they turned their mounts toward the manor. The air was heavy with impending rain when they returned, and Kenric ordered a fresh horse.

"The weather is turning... must you go?" LaVet asked, as she removed Beauty's saddle and started to rub her down.

"I have delayed too long already. A little rain will not do me any harm," he commented, as two of the stable boys took over rubbing down the horses.

"All right," She fell into step with Kenric as they headed toward the house. "I should dress then see if Grandmother needs anything. She seems to be awfully worn since the ball." LaVet glanced up as she walked next to Kenric. He was staring at her from the corner of his eye with an expression she had never seen before.

"What is it? Is something wrong?" she pressed.

Kenric shook his head slightly. "You called her 'Grandmother'; not Lady Maren-- not referring to her as only *my* relation. I think it will please her."

Something unspoken passed between them then, a feeling of kinship that hadn't been there before. A mutual love of Lady Maren and concern for her welfare was connecting them in a way northing else previously had.

***

Lady Maren walked slowly at LaVet's side as the two women traversed the family portrait gallery. She had insisted that the two of them take a turn around the house while the rain poured down outside, and after a few days in bed asserted the exercise would do her good.

Every few steps Lady Maren would point to a portrait and share the name of the person looking out at them, passing on bits of information and stories.

"This is *my* Nicolas. He was such a good and handsome man." LaVet raised her eyes to the painting of Kenric's grandfather.

"Kenric has his eyes." LaVet observed the deep set grey eyes that were now so familiar to her.

"Yes, such expressive eyes, all their emotions displayed in their depths," Lady Maren sighed. "I see Nicolas each time I look at Kenric." Raising a hand she softly ran the tips of her fingers across the embossed edge of the frame then, dropping her hand back to her side, moved a few feet further down the hall.

LaVet followed for a few steps then lifted her eyes to a second painting. The expert brush strokes and vibrant colors captured a couple she knew without confirmation was Kenric's mother and father.

"They look happy," she mused.

"We have been blessed in this home. Love has been prevalent in relationships that all started out in different forms." Lady Maren smiled sadly.

"The same cannot be said for many, to my understanding. Most couples never truly find that kind of companionship when they marry for fortune, title, position, status or any one of the myriad of reasons for unions." LaVet now felt her own sadness as she reflected on her marriage.

Lady Maren reached to pat LaVet on the arm. "There are indeed many couples who do not find their happiness in each other," she agreed. "Do not allow the beginning of your marriage to define you, my dear. This is your life; you decide the ending. My suggestion is to make it one worth your while." LaVet understand her meaning and hoped she would be able to take the words to heart.

"Lady Maren, how old was Kenric when his parents passed away?"

"Just over eleven years old. It was a very dark time for him. He worshiped them both and was very lost without them."

"So young… I am glad that he had you," LaVet commented with a grateful smile.

"We had each other." The two had started to walk again and LaVet found herself considering the woman next to her. She was intelligent, strong and didn't mold to the conventions of others. LaVet supposed for all of this she should also be thankful. If not for Lady Maren's influence and hand in raising Kenric, her own life now might be very different.

LaVet felt a rush of gratitude toward Lady Maren. She had prepared Kenric for life with such a rash and unconventional woman as herself. He was open and kind to her, treating her as an equal and with respect; all traits not commonly held by the high born in regard to their wives.

"Do you know how the feud between our families started?" Lady Maren asked, as LaVet fell back into step next to her.

"Truly, I never felt obliged to ask," she answered honestly.

"I can understand. The incident took place generations before your birth. It would make sense to feel as though it has no relevance to your life now. I know that is how I felt when I learned of the history."

"Can you tell me about it?" LaVet pressed.

"Our families where once nothing more to each other than acquaintances, who happened to pass each other in society's circles while on holiday in Bath," Lady Maren said as they walked. "One family had two sons. The firstborn met a young woman at an assembly and fell wildly in love with her. The woman in question was betrothed to another.

"Unable to bear the thought of being forever separated, by marriage to a man she didn't know, they eloped. Her betrothed was outraged by the slight and she was disowned by her family."

"And her husband?"

"Disinherited; everything passed to the younger son. My great, great, great grandfather."

"What happened to the couple?" LaVet enquired.

"Not much is known about them. Their names ceased to be spoken; their marriage went unacknowledged by their families. And as the years passed the bad blood between both families became so deeply rooted that those living on the estates began to fight. Any farmer living on the Leighton estate would spit upon a farmer from the Roche estate. Sons would duel for the honor of their households and each was taught to hate the other. The reasons faded, but the anger and animosity remained.

"A few attempts were made at peace. Tracts of land that used to touch were sold by both families to separate the great estates, in hopes that distance would soon solve the problem. This was a temporary cure to a larger problem. There was a deep-seeded sense of having been dishonored in both great families, and neither could move past it. I believe this is why your great-grand father sold his estate and purchased another, larger estate farther away; the one your father now holds."

"All of this over a marriage?" LaVet asked, in disbelief.

"My dear, if your marriage helped to end it, does it seem so impossible to believe that a marriage could have started it?"

"I… did my marriage really broker peace on more than paper?"

"In recent memory we had moved past the dueling, but the mutual hatred remained until well after my husband passed from this life. My son felt it was a waste of time to hold such a petty grudge that no longer affected anyone living. He reached out to your father years ago. The two agreed to work in unison to discourage any further fighting among those who lived on their lands and at a future time to join the families in marriage."

"A betrothal?" LaVet breathed.

"Of sorts. I don't believe your father had any intention to marry you to Kenric at the time. It very well may have been intended to fall on the next generation. Then you came of age, and my grandson had yet to attach himself to anyone..."

"A marriage of convenience." LaVet said the words aloud but it was more to herself then to Lady Maren.

"In the end it had the desired effect," Lady Maren mused.

"I suppose so," LaVet agreed, then thought to ask, "Do you know the names of the couple that eloped?"

"David and Dawn-Anna."

***

While Lady Maren set herself to her needlework, LaVet penned a letter to her father asking if he had any knowledge of Dawn-Anna and David. She told him of her conversation with Lady Maren and what she had learned concerning them. Then her pen slowed and she held it above the paper, wondering how to continue.

She left the writing table and strode to the window, watching the torrents of rain pouring outside.

"The rain will not keep Kenric away long," Lady Maren said with a reassuring tone and patted LaVet's hand.

"I am concerned for him, riding in such a torrent as this. Even those in the very best of health have fallen gravely ill in such cold, wet conditions." LaVet took a take up post at the window and kept her vigil there for several hours.

As the daylight faded Lady Maren set her needlework aside and, seated close to the fire, soon nodded off.

Just when LaVet was on the verge of tears with worry the sound of pounding hooves reached her ears. Her eyes strained for the sight of the rider through the sheets of rain and dimming evening light.

She sighed with deep relief when the form of a man came into view. She knew in the next instant that it was not Kenric, and fear for the news carried by the rider gripped at her heart.

Riding hard, the horse kicked up gravel in a spray when reined in near the front door. The rider was met by one of the footmen, who took the rains as the rider dismounted.

Hearing the door shut hard and male voices she readied herself to receive the visitor. She didn't have to wait long. The door to the small sitting room burst open and Fitzroy flew in. He looked wild; soaked through and dripping wet.

"Sir Fitzroy!" she stammered in utter surprise.

"Lady Leighton, I beg pardon for my intrusion. Your man informed me that Kenric was away from home. Is that true?"

"I'm afraid so. He was supposed to be home today, but I fear the rain has postponed his return," she explained.

"Damn," he muttered, and slapped his hat on his leg, sending a torrent of water to pool at his feet.

"May I be of any assistance?" LaVet asked, with real concern.

"You? No, the aid of a female is of no use to me." Fitzroy snapped in clear frustration. Trying not to take offense, she indicated to an open chair.

"Please, won't you come in and dry yourself near the fire while you wait for him?"

Fitzroy seemed to think on this for a moment then sighed heavily. "I will take a glass of brandy and a fresh horse if you can spare it."

"You cannot be thinking of riding out at this hour and in this storm, surely?"

"I must go." He bowed his head to her and turned swiftly to leave.

"Wait!" she called out. "Please, I will make sure a horse is ready for your use and whatever else you require." She gestured toward the fire. "Warm yourself, Fitzroy, while I send for the stable boy."

He looked at her with clear distrust and moved to stand near the fire.

LaVet rushed from the room to see to the preparations for his departure.

Turning a corner she encountered Frances. Not giving her the chance to express her surprise, she instructed the maid to take brandy to Sir Fitzroy along with some meat and cheese.

As an after thought LaVet added that she should fetch a dry coat from Kenric's manservant.

Then she hastened to see to the fresh horse. Once assured that the stable hands had the addling underway, she returned to the small sitting room to find Fitzroy greedily eating while Frances poured him a drink.

"The horse will be ready shortly-- however, I must ask yet again, won't you consider staying? At least until Kenric returns?"

"There is no help for me here," Fitzroy snapped, swiftly leaving the room.

LaVet watched from the window as the fresh horse was led up to the house. Fitzroy grabbed angrily at the reins, pulling them sharply out of the stable boy's hands, mounted the animal then pounded away, the rain distorting his form.

Once she was no longer able to see him she turned back to the fire and a sleeping Lady Maren, all the time wondering what could possibly have been the matter?

***

"Did I do the right thing by giving him the horse and not insisting he stay?" LaVet asked, after she had finished relaying her story of Fitzroy's unexpected visit of the night before.

"Yes, of course you did. There would have been no way to stop Fitz from leaving, even if you had wished to. It is better he had a fresh horse." Kenric rubbed at his temple, the effects of little sleep lingering.

"Do you have any idea what could possibly have driven him out this far in such weather looking for you?" she asked, and waited as Kenric rolled the question over in his mind.

"I have some idea but it's only a suspicion, and until I have more information I don't feel that I can speak for Fitz."

"I understand." she reassured him. "I do hope, whatever it is, that everything will be all right."

"In point of fact, I have received news of a happier sort," Kenric noted, and placed his water glass back down on the table. "Caroline Ludlow has been married."

The news took LaVet aback a moment.

"Caroline is married?"

"Yes, it seems that once she was removed from her father's home Caroline warmed to the idea of acquainting herself with the man she was intended to marry in the first place. Only weeks later the wedding took place. She is now Mrs. Doyle, and by all accounts is very happy."

"Poor Peter," LaVet said sadly.

"Is he?" Kenric asked, one eyebrow raised. "Or, is he lucky?"

"What do you mean?"

"Peter Decker may now be disheartened, but in time I believe he will come to understand that marriage to a woman who is so easily persuaded to believe her self in love, and just as easily to think herself out of love in such a short span of time would have made him a very unhappy man."

LaVet thought over his assessment. "I have been thoroughly censured and will remember my place in attempting to advise you on such subjects in the future. I was utterly wrong."

Kenric looked at her with concern. "LaVet, this is not a reprimand. Like Peter and Caroline, you and I can walk away from this experience having learned something. I learned to listen to all concerned, and if I hadn't, Caroline's reputation could have been ruined by false accusations. Peter would have been labeled a rake and a seducer, and neither would have been able to avoid total scandal."

"I should apologize to you. That was unfair... I have grown disposed to act defensively over the years with my father's tactics to persuade me to behave better. I should not have tried to use guilt or self-contempt as a weapon; it was a childish thing to do." She was looking down at her lap, one hand holding to the necklace at her throat.

"It seems you have learned more than I would have expected from this instance," he said, and cast a smile in her direction.

"I'm afraid I need quite a lot of improvement still. I have so many disagreeable faults. I am sure you will soon grow tired of becoming aware of them... long before they are all discovered." LaVet attempted a laugh.

"My dear wife. You have fewer than you believe, in my eyes."

***

My most cherished brother,

I was more pleased than I can express to receive your last letter. It had been too long since I had heard from you. To know you are well puts my fears to rest. Both Kenric and I were glad to learn of your swift ascent through the ranks of the royal navy, although I cannot express the same joy over you being sent so far away. The West Indies seem so incredibly removed. Please promise me that you will look after yourself and come back to us complete.

As to your query, I am well. I am able to fill much of my time and do not find myself idle as I had once feared. I am blessed with the friendship of our pastor's wife and the opportunity to serve those who live in Tredan and the surrounding farms.

As the Christmas holidays grow closer I find that I miss my family more than I thought possible. Father's insistence on fresh cranberries and family dinners with all the trimmings are both things I didn't think I would miss, and now recall fondly. Of course, what I miss the most is your company. Write as often as you can and tell me all about your travels.

With all my love, your sister,

LaVet

"Ma'am, my apologies for the interruption. Lord Leighton has asked that you meet him in his study as soon as possible," Collingwood said formally, as he stood in the doorway of the large sitting room.

LaVet placed her letter aside and stood to follow him.

"LaVet, please won't you come in?" Kenric met her at the door of his study and stepped aside to allow her to pass. LaVet moved past him but didn't take a seat as she waited for Kenric to indicate whether or not she should, and what he had summoned her to discuss.

"I have received a letter, the contents of which I feel as though I must share with you. " Kenric moved to hold out a chair for her then took the one opposite.

"You have me a little anxious, has someone been hurt?" she pressed, noting the grim look on his face.

"Do you remember me telling you the story of a young man who had married for love; and that affection was not returned by his spouse?" he asked, looking grave.

"Yes, I remember. Didn't he lose most of his wealth upon their marriage as well?"

"He did. That same man was ruined by this relationship in more ways than one. She has left him, abandoned their children, and taken all that was left of his fortune. They are now destitute and will soon be without a home, it will be sold to pay against the outstanding debts she left behind," Kenric said, with such feeling in his voice that it made LaVet ache inside.

"You're speaking of Alistair Fitzroy, aren't you?" she whispered in despair.

"I am," he confirmed, not lifting his gaze from the floor.

"It was in the manner you spoke; with such sadness," she answered.

"You are very discerning. Fitz informs me that his wife, Valeria, has not merely abandoned them, but has left with another man. They are thought to be in Scotland but he is unable to trace her."

"The evening that… that he rode to the manor. He was searching for her." It was not a question. LaVet felt ill, thinking of how little help she had been to him and how relieved she had been when the awkwardness of their meeting had been over.

"It would seem so."

He got to his feet and started to pace the room. For a hideous moment LaVet felt a sense of helpless desperation grip her.

"Kenric, how much time would Sir Fitzroy need to settle his business in London?" she asked finally, as an idea struck her.

"I'm not sure; his wife has left him with numerous debt collectors now baying for blood. It's bad enough that the sale of his home and any of its finer furnishings will not be sufficient to pay them all off."

LaVet shot from her seat and walked to where Kenric had stopped pacing. "You must help him. Go to London, settle his accounts and bring Fitzroy and the children here," she said in a rush, before the boldness to do so left her.

When Kenric didn't respond she placed a tentative hand on his arm and went on, "Leighton Cottage is now vacant with the departure of the Hooper family, and did you not charge Collingwood with finding new tenants for it some days ago? Sir Fitzroy and his children would be very comfortable there with a few new furnishings, I am sure."

Kenric turned, taking both of her hands in his and stood looking at her for several seconds.

"Are you in earnest?" he pressed.

"Of course. He is your friend; there is no question." Kenric smiled slowly as the words left her lips.

"You are everything that is right with this world," he said, and leaning forward placed a kiss to her brow. LaVet felt the air rush from her lungs and her eyes fluttered shut. The contact was brief and before she was sure it had really occurred Kenric stepped back; her hands now free to dangle uselessly at her sides.

"I should write some instructions for Collingwood and Gallagher before I am away," Kenric commented, sounding a bit out of breath. "Then prepare to depart for London."

"I will make a list of items in the cottage that need repair or replacement, for your approval," she offered.

"I trust your judgment completely. Whatever you feel needs to be done to add to the comfort of his family, please see to it," he said, moving to the desk and making ready to pen a letter.

"Very well." With her head slightly spinning, LaVet made to leave the room. As she reached the door she turned to add, "December cold is no friend to the traveler. Take care, Kenric, to return home safely." His dark head lifted, but before he was able to reply LaVet slipped form the room and closed the door behind her. She then rushed down the hall toward the smaller of the sitting rooms and took up her own pen.

Once seated at her desk she found it difficult to focus on the task; her mind drifting to Kenric's study. Her fingers flittered from the writing materials to the place his lips had rested.

Feeling as though her sister's words to her were mistaken wishes for LaVet's own happiness, she had put little stock into them. It seemed utterly impossible that Kenric could feel anything deeper for her than respect.

The intimate exchange could be nothing more than his way of showing gratitude for her suggestion, and would not soon be repeated. Pushing it out of her mind, LaVet set back to work. Several minutes passed, then Collingwood was tapping at the door.

"My Lady, Lord Leighton has charged me to deliver this to you," he said, and held out a piece of parchment. "He also said that whatever assistance you may require in the venture he left for you, I am to be at your full disposal. Please, do not hesitate to call on me." Collingwood bowed slightly at the waist as she took the parchment from his hand.

The page was filled with Kenric's heavy scrawl.

My dearest LaVet,

As I wrote instructions out for Collingwood, a few things came to mind. First, although, I know you will look after Grandmother during my absence, I fear I do not have time to take proper leave of Grandmother, as she is away from the manor this afternoon.

Would you give her my condolences and assurance that I will make every attempt, God willing, at a speedy return.

Second, I will correspond with you from London but for now I must ask that you add to your considerable task of preparing the cottage for Fitzroy's family; finding a suitable governess for the children.

I leave you this very delicate task knowing it will not be easy with Fitzroy's distrust of any member of the female sex. I fear he will have become even more difficult with the betrayal by his wife and he will not act with kindness toward whomever is placed over the care of his children.

Both Collingwood and Gallagher will be at your disposal. I will try and return before Christmas day.

Yours faithfully,

~Kenric

***

Lady Maren shifted in her seat next to LaVet in the carriage and shoved her hands into the fur muff on her lap.

"I detest this infernal cold," she muttered, as the driver started the horses for home. "I do believe it's much colder this winter than last."

LaVet agreed as she pulled her wrap closer around her shoulders. "The service today was well worth braving the cold for."

"Yes, every so often Pastor Long surprises me," Lady Maren allowed, and the two women shared a smile.

LaVet glanced out the window, frowning at the freshly fallen flakes. "Do you believe the weather will delay Kenric's return with Fitzroy?"

"It will make it more challenging to travel comfortably, but he will try his best to keep his promise to you and return by Christmas," Lady Maren reassured LaVet.

"I'm concerned that we haven't heard from him. It's been two weeks," LaVet commented.

"I am sure everything will be fine. How is refurbishing the cottage coming along?"

"Well, the beds have been re-stuffed, the chimneys cleaned and the sitting room sofa recovered. Yet my list keeps growing as more items are found to be in sadder condition than I had anticipated. I do hope to have the house ready when they arrive."

"I am sure you will, my dear."

"Can you tell me anything about the children? I did not think to ask Kenric before his departure," LaVet asked.

"Oh yes, there are two; both girls. The eldest is five now, I believe... her name is... Kathryn. I have not seen her since her birth. The youngest, Shirleen, is now only two years of age." She lowered her voice. "I am told Fitzroy has suspicions that she is not his natural child."

LaVet wasn't sure if she could endure any more news regarding Fitzroy that was so disheartening. The more she learned of his circumstances, the more guilt ate away at her insides. She had never warmed to the man and wondered at her narrow-mindedness in judging him so harshly.

"Fitzroy is no longer the boy I knew in his youth. He has become bitter and angry, allowing Valeria and her betrayal to utterly ruin him and the man he could have become. I suppose I have been terribly unfair to him all these years," Lady Maren voiced.

The carriage stopped and both women retreated to the welcome warmth of the house.

Lady Maren insisted she would not be able to be rid of the December chill until a hot bath had been drawn for her, and was escorted to her chambers. LaVet also retreated to her rooms and sank into a seat near the fire.

"Shall I draw you a bath before I lay out your dress for dinner?" Frances asked, as she built up the fire. The white flurries of snow that glided by the window had captured LaVet's attention. She shook her head at the question and tried to gather herself.

"I'm sorry Frances, my thoughts have taken me elsewhere."

Frances stood and moved from the fire to stand near LaVet. "Is there anything I can help you with, ma'am?"

"Thank you for the concern; I am well." Then LaVet looked more closely at Frances, suddenly seeing her clearly.

"Frances, please come and sit down. I'd like to talk to you." Frances paused, a dark red sash in her grasp and looked at LaVet.

"Have I done something to displease you?"

"No, of course not!" LaVet protested. "Please come sit down with me."

Still looking apprehensive, Frances took the offered seat and sat stiffly facing LaVet.

"There is something on my mind that I wish to speak to you regarding." LaVet cleared her throat. "As you no doubt have heard, Sir Fitzroy and his children will be coming to live in Leighton Cottage."

"Yes."

"I have been charged with finding a suitable governess for his children."

"How can I help?" Frances questioned, and LaVet smiled warmly at her.

"I have spent several days contemplating who might fill this position. There is only one clear choice-- you, Frances."

"Me?" she asked, in utter disbelief. "No, I am no governess, I am a lady's maid."

"I know that being *my* lady's maid has been more challenging than anyone could have anticipated, but you have always risen to the occasion." LaVet sat forward and took both of Frances' hands in hers. "You are an intelligent, kind and strong woman; all qualities that are highly prized... and there is no one else I can ask or trust to take on the task."

Frances was deep in thought for several moments. LaVet cleared her throat and pressed on. "You don't have to answer directly, and although I have faith that you will be the best fit... You are a rare jewel, Frances, and I am loath to lose you as my companion, but never as my friend!" LaVet felt her voice catch and the two women embraced.

***

Christmas dawned bright and crisp. A heavy layer of new snow had fallen during the night, blanketing the trees in silvery white crystals that shimmered and reflected the light of a new day.

LaVet felt a deep melancholy at the sight, Kenric had only written once during his absence, and the letter contained little information besides his well-being and gave no indication of when he might return.

After dressing, she met Lady Maren for a hearty breakfast. The older woman worked hard at keeping LaVet in conversation and her spirits light. It worked as a distraction until Pastor and Mrs. Long came and enlisted LaVet to aid them in delivering last minute bundles to a few Tredan families. LaVet was grateful for the outing and offered the use of one of the Leighton carriages.

Once all the bundles had been delivered and holiday wishes had been exchanged, LaVet found herself alone in the carriage as it carried her home… home; she was going home, wasn't she? It was a miraculous realization. She *was* going home. The manor was no longer just a residence, her husband's home. It was no longer just a symbol of the life she felt she had given up. This place, these people, they had become so much more to her.

~ Chapter Twelve ~

LaVet could feel her spirits dampening as the days passed with no word from Kenric on his expected return. All too soon almost a fortnight had passed. LaVet found herself sitting through a particularly dull sermon, trying uncommonly hard to not yawn. If the truth be told, the sermon might have been exceptional, but her mind was elsewhere and it was impossible for her to notice anything outside of herself.

A hymn was sung with a half-hearted effort and then she bowed her head with the rest of the congregation as the closing benediction was given.

"Lady Leighton." Mrs. Long greeted her as LaVet made her way toward the exit. She returned the warm greeting then addressed Pastor Long.

"Thank you for the sermon."

He smiled warmly at her. "Please give Lady Maren our warmest regards," he said, inclining his head in a small bow of respect.

"I will, thank you."

"I did notice her absence. Is she very ill?" Mrs. Long pressed, with a look of dismay.

"No, not very. However, I am sad to report that the cold does not agree with her."

"I am sure she is keeping the Lord in her thoughts on this day of rest, no matter the mortal condition." Mrs. Long smiled, added, "The excessive cold always keeps a few from venturing out this time of year."

"Yes, I believe it does," LaVet agreed.

"We won't keep you from your carriage any longer, Lady Leighton," Pastor Long said as the line of people ahead of her thinned, each waiting for their own carriages to pull up outside the large double doors before they descended the stone stairs.

"Thank you." She smiled at them both then, pulling her cloak tightly around her, she moved toward the open door of the carriage.

The driver took her by the elbow and helped her into the carriage, where LaVet shivered the duration of the ride back to the manor house, silently wishing she too had the privilege of age to keep her homebound on such a cold day.

The carriage rolled to a stop and LaVet gathered her skirts and was moving to step down when the door swung open to a face she had not expected.

"Kenric!" she said in surprise.

"LaVet." Kenric smiled broadly, then offered her his hand and she took it as he helped her down.

"I was not expecting you." Kenric didn't move to drop her hand. Instead, he placed it in his arm and kept her fingers covered with his own as they walked into the house.

"I would have sent word, but the weather made sending a letter slower than just surprising you with our arrival." he said, with a laugh in his voice.

LaVet wished she was brave enough to tell him that she could not have asked for anything more than his safe return, but the words were caught in her mouth.

A maid rushed to take her cloak and gloves then swiftly disappeared.

"Are you glad to have me back, or too frozen to speak?" he teased, and took her hands in his. "Indeed, you are very chilled. Let's go warm you up near the fire."

Laughter filtered into the corridor from the larger sitting room. The sound was contagious and LaVet found herself smiling before they entered. Fitzroy sat near Lady

Maren, facing the finely decorated mantel piled with brightly wrapped packages, as two fair-haired children played on the carpet with blocks and picture books.

Fitzroy arose at the sight of her. "Lady Leighton, thank you for the invitation." He took her hand and placed a kiss to the back of it.

It was the first time during their meetings he had been even mildly pleasant, and she liked the look on him. "Sir Fitzroy, it is our honor to have you and your children in our home," she said sincerely. A look crossed his face that she wasn't able to quite read, then was gone.

"Let me introduce you." He stepped back and waved the children forward. "This is my eldest, Kathryn." The five-year-old girl gave LaVet a little curtsey. LaVet went to one knee and smiled into her perfectly round face and sweet blue eyes.

"I am very glad to have you here, Kathryn."

"And this is Shirleen." The younger daughter, just as flaxen-haired as Kathryn but with more curls, came to stand next to her sister. She gave LaVet a very practiced reverence and then crinkled her brows together as if displeased. The perfect pink mouth formed a hard line.

"Hello Shirleen, is something wrong?"

The little girl did not look at her father for permission to address LaVet, but rushed forward. "We have been waiting for a very long time for you and father promised us that once you arrived we could finally have some entertainment," the little girl said very decidedly.

"You remind me of your father," LaVet laughed, then realized that the observation had slipped from her lips before she was able to stop it or think through the repercussions. There was an intake of breath and LaVet resisted the urge to glance up at Kenric or Fitzroy.

She straightened. "We've saved Christmas for you. Grandmother and I couldn't bear the idea of celebrating alone. Shall we open gifts?" The two girls squealed with delight as LaVet shepherded them toward the holiday display.

***

Kathryn happily sang carols to entertain everyone assembled as LaVet played the piano. It was truly joyful to hear the sounds of her pure sweet voice ring out. Shirleen was still enthralled with her newest acquisition, a small porcelain doll, and was cradling it softly in her arms.

Collingwood entered to announce that dinner was ready and the levity started to wind down. Frances was then brought into the room and second round of introductions was made. The girls seemed shy and a little reserved when presented to her, and there was an unmistakable look of darkness crossing Fitzroy's features that didn't go unnoticed.

Putting an arm on his friends shoulder, Kenric reassured him that the new governess would be a boon to the girls. "Trust me, when have I ever lied to you?" Fitzroy made no comment as he intently watched the girl's interaction with Frances.

"Are you hungry?" Frances asked them, and both girls gave her their assent.

"Well then, let's go see what cook has prepared for us, shall we?" Frances stood and looked directly at Fitzroy. "If that is all right with you, Sir." With a curtsey she waited for his instruction.

Fitzroy looked from her to Kenric then back and nodded. Frances bowed again and shepherded the children out of the room. Once they were gone Fitzroy turned to

LaVet as she stood from the piano and asked, "May I escort you to the dining hall?"

"Yes," she muttered in surprise, and took his arm. Kenric offered his to Lady Maren and fell into step behind them.

"Would you like to ask me something?" she asked, and Kenric smiled at her openness.

"I'm sorry to be so forward, but did you mean what you said about Shirleen… having a resemblance to me?" LaVet let out a pent-up breath in relief.

"Your… their mother was flaxen-haired as well, I presume," she finally said, stealing a glance over her shoulder. Kenric gave her an encouraging smile.

"She was," he confirmed.

"Hazel eyes as well?" Fitzroy only nodded this time, his jaw clenched.

"It's clear when you look at Kathryn that she takes after both of you, with her mother's fair complexion and your eye color. She also has your chin, nose and ears; features that are clearly yours.

"Shirleen, on the other hand, although sharing some of the same features as her sister, does not clearly mimic your more dominant features. Although her eyes are hazel in color there is a crinkle at the edges and an almost permanent crease in her brow. Both instantly reminded me very much of you and your… scowl. She also purses her lips in the very same manner I have witnessed in you on more than one occasion." she added carefully.

Fitzroy seemed to think about this for several moments. "In truth?"

"It is my observation. And if it helps to ease your mind, I am the only child of three that takes after my father in complexion and countenance." Kenric was impressed with her remarks. However, he knew that if Fitzroy chose not to see himself in his daughter then nothing anyone said would persuade him otherwise.

As they entered the dining hall and took their seats Fitzroy changed the topic. "Tell me more about this governess. I've been assured that whomever you appointed would be more than qualified. What can you tell me about her?"

LaVet illustrated at length on Frances' many qualities until Kenric laughed and said, "You've put the poor man into a daze. He will never believe that such a fine woman can truly exist if you continue to sing her praises."

"I apologize; she is a dear woman and I care for her very much. It is my belief she will be a benefit to your girls, Sir Fitzroy."

"By the way you speak of Frances I have no doubt she will," he replied.

"If it pleases you, I will temper my praise by saying that she is not perfect and has one fault-- or you might find it such,-- that I fear can never be corrected."

"And pray tell what could that be?" Fitzroy asked.

"She has spent too much time with me and feels it is her right to speak her mind. I have been rebuked by her on more than one occasion."

"Yet, a women who knows her own mind and is well educated is welcome to share sound opinions and advice, in times where both are needed," Lady Maren added, and all assembled agreed.

"I only mean, Sir Fitzroy, that I'm afraid Frances will not hold her tongue when she feels that something needs to be said. I have encouraged her in this fault because of her sound advice and friendship. I do hope that you will not look on it unkindly," LaVet implored.

Fitzroy was lost in thought for a moment before answering. "Truly a refreshing flaw. I am glad of it." Kenric listened to the exchange with a growing sense of hope for his friend's future, and a rush of gratitude for LaVet's diplomacy.

***

After Kenric saw to it that Fitzroy and his children were comfortable for the night he retired to the smaller sitting room where LaVet was resting near the fire.

She caught sight of him and sat straighter, "When will you take them to see the cottage?"

"In a few days. The items he was able to bring from London have yet to arrive and I would like to have them there before we introduce the girls to their new home."

"I think that would be best to help their transition," she agreed, as he took the high-backed chair that sat near hers.

"What do you think of the children?"

LaVet smiled. "They seem darling. I do hope this move will not be too hard on them," she added more soberly.

"Fitz has been as honest as possible with them and I have witnessed a great deal of understanding and acceptance from them both. Neither child was a favorite of their mother, nor do I expect they will miss her." Kenric said, with a touch of bitterness.

"She didn't spend much time with them, I presume," LaVet commented.

"As little as she was able, and she changed their governess frequently." LaVet took a long look at him in the firelight as he rubbed the back of his neck and pulled on the loose cravat at his neck.

"You must be tired," she observed.

"I am worn. Do I look it?"

"A night's rest will erase any effects from your travels, I am sure." LaVet felt a yawn forming and pressed a hand to her lips to stave it off.

"It seems we could both use a good rest," he answered, then reached into the pocket of his waistcoat and extracted a small brown package. "Before we retire I'd like to give you this." He deposited it into her hand as she looked at him in disbelief.

"What is this?"

"A Christmas gift."

"Kenric, the new muff you already gave me is more than enough," she protested.

"You must be the only woman on the face of this earth who would argue at receiving gifts. Open it, LaVet," he instructed.

She pulled at the ribbon holding the paper tightly together and pushed back the folds to reveal a small velvet pouch. She tilted the pouch so that two of the most exquisitely formed earrings she had ever seen spilled into her palm.

"Oh, Kenric…" she breathed, and held one up to inspect it more closely. The teardrop shape was encrusted with one large blue sapphire and glittered with small diamonds encircling it in a setting of brilliant gold. "They are exquisite," she finally managed to say.

"You like them, then?" LaVet tore her gaze from the glittering jewels and held her breath momentarily as Kenric's intense storm grey eyes held hers.

"I love them, thank you," she said softly, and felt a rush of heat flood her face that had little to do with her proximity to the fire.

"I'm very glad." There was a low husky tone to his voice that made LaVet cast her eyes back down to her lap as one hand played at the pendant around her neck. She felt strongly that her gift to him of a new watch and chain paled in comparison to his thoughtfulness.

"It's late. Would you allow me to escort you to your chambers?" Kenric asked, after several minutes of silence. LaVet slipped the earrings back into their confinement and nodded.

"Thank you, it's been a very full day. I am more tired than I realized." She gladly took his arm and together they walked toward the family's wing of the house.

"I didn't have the chance to tell you before that I heartily agree with the appointment of Frances as the new governess. You did well there."

"I'm glad you approve."

"Were you able to find a suitable replacement for your lady's maid?" Kenric asked.

"Oh... yes. She is a sweet girl from Tredan. Opal Carlson."

"I know the family. She is a pleasant girl, and I hope that she does well in her new position."

"I believe she will."

"Grandmother informs me that you have exceeded her every expectation in regards to carrying out your duties as the Lady of Leighton Manor. I'm pleased to hear such high praise on your behalf." LaVet felt a rush of pleasure at the clear pride held in his tone.

"I am glad to hear it, although I would be quick to disagree. I am lacking in so many areas that it sometimes feels overwhelming. Grandmother has been a constant source of counsel to me…" Then, glancing up at him, she added with feeling, "Yet, I am so very pleased to have you home."

Kenric slowed his steps as they had reached her chamber door, and releasing her arm turned to look at her. "This whole mess with Fitz has taught me a few valuable lessons, one of which is the importance of having a true partner in this life… someone to rely on and trust." His eyes searched her face in the dim flicker of the lamplight. For a moment it seemed as though Kenric was going to say something more, then he swallowed hard and stood straighter.

She watched in wonder as the flash of his gaze glittered, then died.

"Good night, LaVet." LaVet stood rooted to the spot as she watched his retreating back, and then slipped into her rooms in a daze.

What was it that she saw so often in his gaze that made her heart quicken and stopped her breath? She had missed his company more than she was willing to admit, and upon seeing him again her feelings of longing to be near him would not be denied any longer.

LaVet retreated to her small writing desk tucked away in one corner of the room. There she slid the earrings out and held them in her hand. He had waited to give her this gift until they were alone. There was no fuss or public display to attract compliments on his thoughtfulness. The exchange had been oddly intimate with no onlookers, and LaVet wasn't able to stop wondering if the meaning of the moment held the same significance for Kenric as it had for her.

Octavia,

> *My dearest sister… After your visit I have been daily thinking over our*

conversations in regards to Kenric's feelings for me, as well as mine for him. Although

he is still kind and attentive he is also guarded. Often I feel as though he is holding back

in our exchanges. There have been times... when a glance or smile has made me think

that perhaps he could care for me. Then just as suddenly as the hope appeared, it is

easily abandoned as he becomes distant. And I am afraid I have allowed myself to make a

horrid misstep.

For I have fallen in love with my husband.

~ Chapter Thirteen ~

"Pastor and Mrs. Long, to what do we owe this visit?" Lady Maren asked, gesturing for everyone to take a seat.

"Thank you for having us on such short notice," Pastor Long said with a smile. "We had hoped to see Lord Leighton and take the chance to welcome his friend to Leighton Manor and Tredan."

"I'm afraid Kenric is out with his steward Gallagher on business and Sir Alistair Fitzroy has joined them," LaVet informed them. "Would you like to stay for tea while we wait for their return?"

"That would be lovely." Mrs. Long accepted the invitation with a warm smile.

Pastor Long engaged Lady Maren in a conversation while his wife turned her attention to LaVet.

"It seems too long since you and I have been able to visit. How have you been?"

"I have been well," LaVet reassured her. "And you? How have you been spending your time?"

"Oh, the duties of the clergy never cease. It is a blessed life, but I must confess that I am feeling every bit my five and thirty years," Mrs. Long said, and LaVet noted the slightest darkening of the skin under her friend's eyes.

Reaching out to take one of her hands, LaVet smiled. "It is this cold winter weather. It affects us all. I am sure you will begin to feel better as soon as the first signs of spring begin to appear. Until that time, please let me assist in any duties where I am able, and do please come here at any time to take a few moments of respite."

Mrs. Long looked into LaVet's face with warmth. "You are so kind."

"I'm afraid that if you were not so agreeable, I would not be so kind." This made

Mrs. Long laugh and one hand flew to her stomach and a look of distress crossed her face.

"I'm sorry, I feel a bout of dizziness coming upon me."

"Come, my dear, a breath of fresh air will do you a world of good." Pastor Long

took his wife by the arm and guided her to a door leading out to one of the many private

terraces, and encouraged her to breathe deeply as he opened it for her.

"She is expecting," Lady Maren whispered to LaVet with a knowing smile.

"No, do you think?"

"Oh, most definitely."

"If she is in fact expecting I am very glad for her," LaVet said, with real

happiness for her friend.

At that moment the door opened and trays of small cakes and buttered buns were

brought in along with tea.

Once everyone was served the four sat in relative silence between sips of sweet

peppermint tea and bites of cake, with only a few well-placed compliments on the quality

of the buns and selection of cakes. Then it seemed Mrs. Long remembered something of

particular interest; her eyes growing bright with excitement as she chewed faster,

attempting to hurry and empty her mouth of its contents.

"I almost forgot to relay some very thrilling news indeed!" she said, around a

quick sip of tea. "We have just been informed of an impending wedding! It's all very

exciting because, like your own, it is another great match. Lord Abney has given his

blessing on the marriage of his daughter!"

Mrs. Long talked with such enthusiasm that it took LaVet a few moments to understand that she was speaking of Emmaleen Abney.

"Lady Abney is engaged?" LaVet asked, almost unbelieving.

"Oh yes, to Sir Barnabas Ellsworth. Lady Abney and her father have left for London to purchase her wedding clothes. I am positive that the whole occasion will be magnificent!"

"Will they be married in Tredan?" Lady Maren inquired.

"No, Sir Ellsworth's estate is nearer London and it will take place there. I am afraid we have seen the last of Lady Abney until after she has given up her father's name as well as his house. I do hope to have the pleasure of her company when they come to visit her father, in time. She has always been such a thoughtful and pleasant young woman... and a dear friend of Lord Leighton's!" she added.

"Indeed, we will send her our warmest congratulations," Lady Maren said with a forced smile and a glance shared with LaVet expressing their mutual surprise and relief that Emmaleen Abney was, for the time being, removed far from their lives.

***

"Won't you play for us tonight, my dear?" Lady Maren asked, as Kenric led her into the sitting room.

LaVet looked up from her needlework at the request and hesitated a moment.

"Do, LaVet. I have rarely heard a talent such as yours and it would be a pleasure." Kenric smiled with encouragement.

"Please, do," Kathryn chimed in from her seat on the floor, where the two girls had been busying themselves with looking at a large picture book.

"It is our last night in the manor house, and it would be a very pleasant way to spend the time," Fitzroy added.

"You make it impossible to say no, Sir Fitzroy." LaVet relented and placed her needlework to the side.

"Well then, let's all retire to the music room. There is much better selection of instruments there for her to play upon," Kenric said to the room at large, and walked to LaVet, offering her his arm. They led the way for the small party, Fitzroy escorted Lady Maren while Frances and the children brought up the rear.

"Do you have a request, Lady Maren?" LaVet questioned.

"No, do you Kenric?" His grandmother asked him, and Kenric smiled broadly.

"I do. First, I'll have everyone seated." Kenric instructed Fitzroy to have Lady Maren take a high-backed chair. Each of the others took the remaining chairs on either side of the matriarch. Kenric led LaVet to the pianoforte to take her seat at its keyboard.

"What is your request?" LaVet asked, as she warmed her hands. Kenric retrieved the piece he had been thinking of and handed the sheets to her. She looked them over before nodding, "Very nicely chosen."

Kenric moved to take his place near his grandmother's chair, and with the small assembly enjoyed the song LaVet played; a very lively Mozart piece that highlighted her true talent in its complexities. Then the girls begged Frances to join LaVet for a duet. They proceeded to laugh and squeal in delight at seeing their governess play.

"Lady Leighton, can you also play the harp?" Kathryn asked, with delight.

"She does, in fact, and play very well," Frances offered.

"Would you mind the change?" Lady Maren pressed.

"It has been some time since I have played, but if you all promise not to be too harsh in your judgments then I will."

Kenric watched intently as LaVet moved to the large pedal harp and allowed her fingers to lightly strum the taut strings.

"I'd like to start with the song my father most requested, if that would be all right?"

"Of course," everyone chimed, almost in unison.

Once done, there was a round of clapping and begging from the girls for another.

LaVet obliged with three more masterfully beautiful pieces. The last was slow and melodic. Kenric thought she played with a hint of sadness in her countenance, or was it longing that he saw there?

All too soon it was late and time for Kathryn and Shirleen to retire for the night. Fitzroy excused himself to see his girls off to bed as Frances ushered them out of the room. His grandmother had begun to nod off as well, and Kenric coaxed her from her chair and exited the room, leading her to her chambers.

***

Finding herself alone in the great room with the departure of Kenric and Lady Maren, LaVet moved back to sit back at the pianoforte. Resting her hands on the keys she plucked out a light tune, humming the melody then, after a moment, sang softly. It wasn't until the song was done that she noticed the room was no longer empty.

Her fingers pulled back as if the keys had been set aflame. "Oh! I didn't know I had company."

Kenric had kept his vigil from the door and was now closing the space that separated them.

"I'm glad you didn't notice; I would have been very remiss if you had stopped. You have such a charming voice," he commented in a way that sent her stomach into a flutter.

"Thank you, although I am inclined to disagree."

"And is this the kind of disagreeing that provokes me to argue with you and forces further compliments to be lavished upon you?" he asked, resting one arm on the pianoforte and leaning against its side, looking closely at her.

"No, I am not the kind of woman that hints for compliments. It was a true statement. I do not particularly like to sing and feel that singing in public is not a talent I possess," she answered plainly.

"You are entitled to your opinion, I suppose. Even if it is wrong," he teased.

"As are you," she countered.

"I don't believe I've heard that particular song before. Who is the composer?'

"I am." LaVet answered. "The music alone, the words belong to my mother's favorite poem."

Kenric gazed at her for a long moment. "You continue to surprise me," he said, in a low voice that had taken on a husky quality, sending shivers down her spine. The storm was back in Kenric's gaze.

She was caught, frozen in a moment that stood as still as the air trapped in her lungs, unable to take a breath for fear that the feelings inside her would escape and form into words.

Knowing and acknowledging her own feelings for Kenric changed everything. It was impossible to think clearly when in his presence. Her mind was constantly occupied with thoughts of him. It was torture not to have any notion if he did-- or ever could--return her affection. Yet, how could he? She was nothing to the woman he should have married, and LaVet felt acutely each of her shortcomings as a wife and partner for such a man. She was just a girl after all; a headstrong, obstinate girl, and Kenric deserved more.

"LaVet, are you all right?" Kenric asked, touching her arm and making her realize that she was looking beyond him now, scowling while lost in thought.

LaVet swallowed hard and was saved from having to form a response as Fitzroy joined them at that moment. He commented on the need for a nightcap.

"Yes, I think I could use one as well," Kenric remarked.

LaVet stood. "I will take my leave of you then. Good night." She gave both men a slight bow and started toward the door.

"Allow me to escort you," Kenric called after her.

"There is no need; I am not so tired I cannot see myself to my chambers. Stay with your friend." She didn't wait for his answer but rushed out, glad to not be examined by either man as she attempted to regain some semblance of control over herself.

~ Chapter Fourteen~

The manor house felt larger and desolate with the noticeable absence of Fitzroy, Frances and the girls. It was only five days since their departure for the cottage and LaVet saw them every day, but when she returned to the large stone edifice of the manor she felt as empty as its rooms.

This particular dreary January day kept her inside and, disliking idleness deeply, she sought to lose herself in the library. Seated in one of the overstuffed chairs near a window she read for hours, and this is how Kenric found her.

"Would you care for tea?" he inquired, and then glanced at the book she had open. "Why on earth are you reading that?" The book was lifted from her hands.

"I wanted to know about… well, more about your family. Its history."

"Who married who, the size of the dowry, birth and death dates…" Kenric snapped the book closed and took a seat across from her. "You could have found a much more interesting way of learning about the Leighton legacy."

"I've exhausted Grandmother of all her stories. In fact, she is the one that suggested I come to the library and look over the family ledgers."

"All right, and what have you learned?" he asked, one eyebrow raised.

"Not much more than I already knew," she relented with a laugh.

"You have only exhausted one source."

"What do you mean?" LaVet asked, wondering if she had missed something in her search of the library.

"Myself, of course."

"Oh, I… I had not thought to bother you… I know you must be very busy and I would hate to be one more thing taxing your time." Her hand had flown to her mother's necklace, rolling the pendant between two fingers.

Kenric reached out and pulled her hand away, taking it in both of his, forcing her to look over at him. "I always have time for you."

"Excuse me, my Lord," Collingwood's voice called out clearly into the library. Kenric closed his eyes a moment then answered in an even voice.

"Yes, Collingwood?"

"There is an urgent letter for you." Kenric sighed and released her hand.

Collingwood advanced to offer the letter to Kenric then, bowing low, excused himself and backed out of the room. Kenric looked briefly at the address scrawled across the back of the missive then tore open the seal and read over its contents.

LaVet grew increasingly worried as Kenric's countenance became grave.

"What is it? Truly, you look very troubled," she said with concern.

Kenric looked at her then and his features darkened further. Slowly he folded the letter and seemed to steady himself with a deep breath. "LaVet, the letter is from your father."

"My father? What... what could he have said that would elicit such a reaction from you?"

Kenric shifted in his seat, sliding forward so that he was closer to her. The ledger slid from his lap to clatter forgotten onto the floor as Kenric captured both her hands in his. LaVet tried to pull back, feeling suddenly sick at the ashen look on his face, but he held fast.

"Kenric? What has happened?" The question came out as a plea for some kind of understanding.

"Your father writes to ask me to... to tell you that... that... your brother's ship was caught in a storm off the coast of the West Indies... his name is not listed among the survivors."

"No." LaVet shook her head. "No... No... NO!" she yelled, and tore her hands from his. Then, shakily, she rose to her feet, feeling as though she had to move-- that perhaps wringing her hands would erase what she had just heard. The urge for action, to do something was so overwhelming that she wasn't able to stop her feet from pacing.

"It can't be--not Barton-- there must be some kind of mistake. There must be... something..." She could hear the high panicked pitch of her voice, but the fact that it was her words, or that the words being spoken were coming from her lips, didn't register.

"Your father says he assessed the information twice before sending word to you or Octavia." Kenric's voice reached LaVet as if through a heavy fog.

"No... do not tell me that... do not tell me that Barton is... I must go... I must go to my father." She felt the grip of hysteria seize her as her arms wrapped around her middle, and she rocked back and forth writhing in unfathomable pain.

"LaVet, he is not there. Your father has gone... he is gone to see if he can find out more information. He will contact us as soon as he can." Kenric was standing near her. She was aware of him but wasn't able to fully take in anything he said.

"I... I need..." Her eyes focused on him for a brief moment and she tore the letter from his grasp, rushing to unfold it.

The room spun as she looked over her father's heavy scrawl. "No! Barton... my dear brother... oh, Lord, why?" Tears splashed onto the parchment.

Kenric retrieved the letter from her fingers and dropped it upon a table before pulling her firmly against him. His arms encircled her as she wept freely, tears staining the silk of his waistcoat.

"Shhhh, my love, shhhh." Kenric whispered softly next to her hair, his lips pressed tenderly to the top of her head.

The sobs began then, racking her body with ferocity as they came in powerful waves, leaving her incapable of standing without support. Breathing became impossible as a weight on her chest seemed to be crushing the air from her lungs. Then, with a burst of pain she cried out, "Barton!" before darkness edged its way into her vision.

***

A cold cloth pressed over her eyes was the first thing LaVet became aware of. She tried to command her hands to move and lift it off but they didn't respond. There was a heaviness to every limb of her body that made motion seem impossible.

As she slowly awoke she noted a searing pain behind her eyelids, which felt gritty and painfully dry against her eyes as if she had dirt kicked into them. Her mouth was also dry and her throat hurt when she swallowed.

Regaining her strength, she lifted one hand and grasped the cloth covering her face. Pulling it off, she commanded her eyes to open. The action was uncomfortable and her eyes protested greatly. With the tips of her finger she could feel the swollen and angry skin of her eyelids and knew she must have cried terribly hard to cause such a reaction.

As her blurry vision cleared she was able to recognize items around her and knew she was in her chambers. The hour was late, and the room was aglow with the warmth of the hearth fire.

A movement caught her eye and LaVet rolled her head over on the pillow. Kenric was sitting propped up in a chair at her bedside. He looked disheveled; his stock untied, the neck of the crisp shirt hanging open low over his chest. The waistcoat had been discarded and lay carelessly over the chair arm. She watched him a long moment as his dark head lulled to the side in sleep.

LaVet attempted a dry swallow that ended up in a fit of coughing. The sound roused Kenric, who sat up straight then bolted from his chair.

"LaVet..." He was at her side faster than she would have imagined possible.

She swallowed uncomfortably. "Water...please."

"Of course, love. Here, let me help you sit up." She felt the strength of his arm behind her shoulders, supporting her as a cup was pressed to her lips. The cool liquid poured over their cracked surface and she gulped at it greedily.

"How are you feeling?" Kenric addressed LaVet, as he lowered her back to the cradle of pillows.

"As well as I must look," she groaned.

Kenric sat at the edge of her bed so that he was facing her. "You gave me quite the shock," Kenric said, and pushed her hair away from her face, tucking strands behind her ear.

"I'm sorry..." she muttered, as memories started to rush back with painful clarity.

"I've never been so scared as the moment you went limp in my arms." The emotion in his words pulled at her heart and a new wave of emotion threatened to overtake all rational thought.

"How long... how long have I been asleep?" she asked.

"Several hours. You... you were weeping for most of that time," Kenric said with a touch of sadness.

"It's real then... and not a nightmare?" she asked, her voice breaking.

Kenric nodded then grasped one of her hands in his. "What can I do? Is there anything you could possibly require of me that might bring you some amount of comfort?"

LaVet knew she wouldn't be able to respond and pursed her lips together to stop them from trembling. Even in her current state of despair she recognized Kenric's own distress. The look of concern she saw in his face was touching and painful. Slowly she shook her head.

"You should rest," he muttered, and moved to stand. On impulse she gripped his hand tighter.

"Don't go..." she whispered. "Please, I don't want to be alone."

Kenric studied her for a moment then settled himself next to her, his long legs stretched out along the top quilt that covered her, and LaVet was gathered closely to his side as one arm cradled her. She rested her head in the crook of his shoulder where she fell fast asleep, listening to the sound of his heart beating.

***

LaVet watched from behind the writing desk as Kathryn and Shirleen happily played a game; their dolls held tightly as each cooed and fussed over them. The sound of pure joy as the children giggled brought a lightness to her heart she had not known in months.

"I am glad to be back," she heard Fitzroy say to Kenric, as he took a seat on a low sofa near where his children entertained themselves.

"It looks as if your daughters are glad as well," Kenric commented.

"I did miss them both terribly." LaVet let her eyes wander to the men. Fitzroy had been to London. The attorney that was hired to finalize his divorce had been able to locate Valeria and he had returned from the city a new and free man.

"Do you like your new dolls?" Fitzroy asked, leaning down to catch the children's attention.

"Oh yes, father!" Kathryn jumped to her feet and rushed to hug him. Little Shirleen mimicked her sister's eagerness and also tossed herself into her father's arms. He hugged them both back and placed a kiss on the tops of their heads before insisting they return to play.

LaVet breathed deeply, then turned her eyes back to the letter she had been attempting. Looking over it, every word sounded insipid to her. Crumpling it up and tossing it aside, she prepared a new parchment. It was difficult to know what to write back to her sister. Putting her feelings or thoughts to paper seemed impossible.

Twelve weeks had passed since news of Barton's fate had reached her; twelve weeks that blended together into one dull memory of nothingness. She could not recall what she had worn the day before or if she had eaten that morning. Each day merely bled into the next without end.

There had been an additional letter; she could recall its contents with perfect clarity. Her father had confirmed that Barton was not one of the twelve that had survived, and he was now ranked as "lost at sea". She was informed that there would be a service held for the family when the weather permitted travel over such a distance. He expressed his great sorrow and love for his remaining children.

She had not been able to cry over the words contained in his letter. There were no more tears, no more shouting, no appeals of "why?" or expressions of utter pain. LaVet felt herself only a shell. Grief had taken everything from her and the woman that remained was nothing.

Surrendering her efforts on Octavia's letter, LaVet placed the pen down and pushed back her chair. The action brought her the room's attention.

"Excuse me," she whispered, and slipped from the room. Although it was the first week of April signs of winter still clung to the ground and there was no place of retreat. So LaVet wandered the halls, seeking solace in the peace they offered.

As she often had, she found herself in the portrait hall, looking over faces of people she had never met.

"My lady, may I join you?" Frances asked, as she fell into step with LaVet, who didn't answer.

"This is a part of the house I don't believe I have seen before." Frances commented. Again LaVet made no effort to reply.

Frances turned sharply to face her and stopped their progress. "LaVet, may I speak openly to you?"

"I suppose I won't be able to stop you," she droned dully.

"Did you know that I lost my sister when we were both young?" Frances asked.

LaVet lifted her eyes in surprise. "No." She realizing she had never asked her former lady's maid any personal questions about her past.

"Yes, she and I had taken my father's horse and gone riding. At twelve and ten respectively we knew better than to take the animal without a guide or our parents' knowledge, but Molly was a lot like you; wild and free." Frances smiled sadly at the memory.

"Something spooked the horse and it threw us. I landed hard in the grass, knocking the air from my lungs. When I was able to regain my senses I crawled to where my sister lay. Her head had hit a rock, and no matter how much I pleaded she would not wake." Tears glistened in her eyes and LaVet watched as they now spilled down her face, unabashed.

"I had no idea..."

"I wish to tell you this as a friend, LaVet. You are not alone in your pain. In this very house are people who have lived with the kind of loss you now suffer. We care for you and wish to help, but you have locked each of us out."

"I... I can't talk about... it's too hard." Heated emotion rose in her chest like bile.

"You do not have to speak of Barton," Frances reassured her. "Just be careful not to stop living while you're still alive. You know it's not what your brother would have wished for you and you have friends here." Frances leaned in and placed a kiss to LaVet's cheek and, with skirts twirling, turned and left her alone to think on the words Frances had imparted.

***

Frowning, LaVet pulled up the horse. Gathering her skirts, she leapt down from the chaise into the soft earth and assessed the road ahead of her. A succession of rainy days had melted a large amount of snow and ice, leaving the roads into Tredan a maze of muddy holes.

The trees grew close on either side of the narrow passage, making navigating this particularly large puddle more difficult than the last few she had encountered. LaVet went back to the chaise and taking the horse by the reins, led the large animal and carriage off to one side of the road to allow other passerby a clear path.

She resolved to finish the short distance on foot. Only moments later she could hear the sounds of approaching hoof-beats and the unmistakable rattle of carriage wheels. Before the carriage was able to pass by other sounds met her ears; the neighing of a frightened horse and a man's voice speaking angrily.

"What have you done!" the deep voice bellowed.

"I do apologize, sir, there was no way to tell…" The other voice was abruptly cut off as the air snapped with the sound of a thud. LaVet felt a vague impression she should not venture further and for a moment stopped, wondering what to do.

As she mulled over her next course of action the sound of another thud and the painful yelp of a man in distress reached her ears.

"Sir…" Thud. "Please…" Whack!

"You useless boy! Look what you have done!" the deeper voice growled, and something deep inside LaVet seemed to break. She rushed headlong past the bend in the road ahead and toward the sounds, heedless of any danger to her own person, and burst onto the scene only a few feet away from a large carriage which had driven right into the very large puddle that was much deeper than it innocently appeared.

The wheel had sunk deeply into the soft earth and one side of the carriage sank low into the brown earth, tilting dangerously. It looked as though at any moment the whole of the carriage would spill into the mud, dragged down by its own weight and overturning the very frightened-looking team of horses.

The animals nickered and dug their hooves into the ground, trying desperately to free themselves from the harnesses that tethered them to the tilting carriage which continued sinking deeper into the large puddle. It appeared the driver had jumped to one side when the wheels became lodged, and that is where his master had found him. She could clearly see two men. One finely dressed, large and red-faced person was screaming at a much smaller man who was cowering in fear, as he had been thrown to the ground and was enduring a beating.

Again and again the large man caned across the back of the man who must have been his driver. Unable to fend off the brutal attack, the small man curled into a ball and threw his arms over his head, only to be kicked hard with the heel of his master's boot, then beat about the head with two sequential raps.

LaVet felt anger flare like wild fire inside her, and calling out, moved as fast as the sodden earth would allow toward the two men. "Please, sir, there is no need to behave so. Your man could not have known how deep this puddle is, or that it would catch your wheels," she protested.

The red-faced man turned on her, surprised at her sudden appearance.

"This is none of your concern," he growled in dismissal, and turned back to deliver, a hard rap to the still cowering driver's exposed back, followed swiftly by a kick to his middle.

"Sir!" LaVet cried, and rushed to throw herself between the large man and his driver. "This can be easily remedied if we work to calm the horses," she said, attempting to reason with the man who only seemed to become redder. Narrowing his eyes, he leered down at her.

"It seems no one has taught you to show respect to your betters and not interfere in the business of others." One beefy hand shot out and shoved her hard to the side. LaVet landed on her knees in the mud.

"I suppose I have time to teach both of you a lesson." He turned from her and went back to his ranting's.

The man held the cane aloft screaming, "You useless… insignificant…wretch!" The cane never made it to its intended target. LaVet had taken up a sturdy branch and now wielded sword, striking the cane aside.

"What on earth?" the man spluttered, then his eyes narrowed dangerously.

LaVet knew the blow was coming before she saw the cane swinging through the air, and as clearly as if he was standing next to her she could hear Barton's voice. "Do not allow your attacker to gain the upper hand." Instinct took over and LaVet lifted her branch, letting the wood take the brunt of the attack.

"Oomph!" the large red face blurted.

His shock didn't last and again she was staving off a blow from his cane. Again LaVet could hear her brother's instructions. "Advance, do not give up your ground!"

It only took moments for LaVet to discover his fighting style and to remember her lessons on how to counteract each move. Suddenly she was near her childhood home, taking swordplay lessons from Barton and besting him, her movements fluid and practiced.

The red-faced man cursed her as LaVet deflected his cane and advanced. He was forced to stumble backward. She saw her opening to disarm the man and took it. With a few well-placed hits the cane flew from his hand and into the mud. The large man was unable to keep his footing and also flew backward, landing hard on his backside in the puddle and sending a wave rippling which caused the horses to rear up.

LaVet kept the branch clutched in one hand and in a calming tone talked to the frightened animals, trying to soothe them. Her efforts were made almost impossible by the sputtering and sloshing of their owner as he disengaged himself from the muck.

The door to the carriage flew open and the voice of a woman called out, "Barnabas?"

"Shut the door and stay inside the carriage! Bloody woman!" The man snapped, clearly livid with her appearance.

LaVet, still trying to calm the horses, had a clear view of the woman that had opened the door and poked her head out of the carriage to assess the situation.

"Lady Leighton…" Emmaleen gasped at the sight of her.

"Emmaleen?" LaVet uttered, in shock at the sight of her. The beautiful woman she remembered had changed drastically, her complexion ashen and now dull eyes rimmed with dark circles.

"Leighton? Of Leighton Manor?" he questioned, his voice still sounding irate.

"Yes, Barnabas, this is the Lady LaVet Leighton." She looked from the large man to Emmaleen, then back. The man she now realized was Barnabas Ellsworth had started to return to a normal color as he stood deep in the muck, staring at her with an open mouth.

"Pardon me, my Lady, I… I had no idea."

"Would you have behaved more like a gentlemen if you had?" LaVet questioned.

Barnabas let out what sounded like a low growl. "You walked into a situation you knew nothing about and made a judgment that was not yours to pass," he countered.

"Senselessly beating a man for what was clearly an accident-- one that could have been easily remedied by now if it weren't for your own action-- was the correct judgment? You acted rashly and foolishly," LaVet retorted.

"You would hold your tongue if you knew what was good for you." Barnabas advanced and LaVet held out the branch at arms length, keeping him at bay.

"Let me remind you, Sir Ellsworth, that I have just bested you and you are now unarmed. As this is not a sword, I have little issue with using it to put you back in your place if you take one step closer." LaVet sounded more confident that she felt, but held her ground.

Barnabas narrowed his eyes then called over his shoulder, "John! Get up and help me with these beasts!"

The driver pulled himself to his feet. Covered in mud, dirt and bloodstains he hobbled toward the horses. Ignoring LaVet, Barnabas grabbed the reins of the nearest horse and with his driver worked to dislodge the carriage from the mud.

Not wishing to spend any more time near the horrid man LaVet turned and, casting a last glance at Emmaleen, fled to her chaise. Releasing her own horse she turned her toward home and set off as fast as the soft ground would allow.

***

LaVet sighed as the manor house came into view. The horse seemed to understand her necessity to be within the peace of its high walls and quickened its pace with no urging. Two stable hands dashed out as she entered the outer yard and helped her out. She didn't attempt to explain her disheveled appearance; instead she dashed toward the steps.

Just as she reached the doors they opened and Collingwood stared down at her in horror.

"My Lady!" he exclaimed. "I saw you racing toward the house-- are you all right?"

"Collingwood, has Fitz arrived?" LaVet cringed at the sound of Kenric's voice as he stepped into the hall and caught sight of her.

In an instant he was clutching her shoulders. "What happened to you?" he demanded. Looking more closely at her, Kenric's lips formed a hard line.

"Collingwood, please fetch tea for my wife and have her maid draw a bath." Kenric tucked her under one of his arms and led her to the nearest sitting room, ushering her inside.

Once alone he turned on her, "LaVet, are you all right?"

She nodded.

"Then please, tell me what happened." The look of concern in his eyes made her chest tighten.

"The roads...the roads were very bad... I was on my way to meet with Mrs. Long and I didn't want to take the carriage. The weather has become so nice and... being trapped indoor all winter... I thought it would be fine to drive myself in the chaise."

"Did you overturn the chaise?" he pressed.

"No. I... would it be all right if I sat down? I'm feeling a little lightheaded," she admitted.

Kenric took her to sit on a low sofa and took the space next to her. It was only then that he noticed that she was shaking. Removing his coat, Kenric laid it across her shoulders then left her to begin piling logs into the hearth. Pulling the coat tightly around her, she breathed in his scent and watched as he worked to light a fire.

"Thank you," she whispered, as the first sparks of light crackled to life. Kenric, still bent low coaxing the fire, turned his head to look at her.

"Thank you for... for... being so kind. I have just seen firsthand what my life might have been if you were not the man that you are," she managed, before emotion cut her words off.

"LaVet, you must tell me what sent you home in such a state," Kenric insisted, then added in a tone laced with fear, "My imaginings are far *worse* than you could understand."

Seeing the distress clearly displayed on his face, she rushed headlong into her tale to put to rest whatever dreadfulness his mind was imagining. Kenric listened for several moments before he cursed under his breath and started to pace the room before her.

LaVet pressed on, describing the altercation on the road and her realization of whom she had just humiliated. When she was done she lifted her eyes to Kenric who had listened without interruption. He had stopped pacing and was now just staring at her, his expression unreadable.

He lowered himself onto one knee in front of her and took her face gently in both his hands. "So, the tear in your dress..." She looked down and saw for the first time an angry gash in the fabric.

"I must have caught it on something, I hardly noticed my actions after I left them to return home."

"And you are sure he did not hurt you?"

"He tried to, but no… I am all right. Cold and dirty, yes…" LaVet left the sentence unfinished as Kenric placed a kiss on her forehead, then without preamble pulled her into his arms.

"I don't know what I would have done if he had harmed you in any way." She found it impossible to speak as Kenric pressed a kiss to her temple and smoothed out her ruffled hair, pushing it away from her face. It was physically impossible for her to draw her gaze away from him as she studied the storm that raged in the depths of his eyes.

LaVet shivered again; not due to the cold clinging to her skin but from the emotion welling up inside of her at his nearness… his touch. He had kissed her twice. The feel of his hands still caressing either side of her face was having the most incredible effect on her pulse as well as on her ability to think in a rationally way.

"Did you really fight him off with a tree branch?" There was the slightest twitch of his lips as he asked the question.

"I'll have you know I am very proficient with a tree branch." She felt the faintest of smiles tilt her lips upward.

"I do not doubt it. I only wish I could have seen you sending that man into the filthy water. To have witnessed the look on his face when he realized who you are, and the sight of that cowardly dog leaving with his tail placed firmly between his legs."

"I'm afraid I have wounded his pride; a deed which is worse to great men than if I had physically harmed him. Do you think he will challenge you?"

"No, Ellsworth has a reputation of being loud, rude and for having a temper. And although he also does not lack for self-love, I doubt he will admit to anyone that he engaged in an altercation with a mere woman and lost. In challenging me to save face he would do the very opposite.

"He will act according to his nature after such an humiliation. I do not believe he will stay long in this part of the county and, with luck, you and I will never cross paths with him again. If I do, I cannot promise you I will not part his head from his shoulders."

"I've never seen such cruelty. He had no remorse... poor Emmaleen... to live with such a man! You do not think... that he could be hurting her?" LaVet shuddered, remembering the shell of the confident woman she had once seen offering to become Kenric's mistress.

"It's best not to think about such things."

"Kenric! If Emmaleen is being abused shouldn't someone do something to stop it?" LaVet said in shock.

"I'm afraid it is not that simple. If I accused her husband, even with proof, unless she is willing to leave him, to become divorced, there is little anyone can do. Emmaleen has always been a woman of means. To divorce would leave her destitute. Her father would never allow her to return to his home; it would be seen as a disgrace, never to be overcome.

"There is also the chance that if she sought refuge with family or friends they would not take her in. Fear of being tainted by association is too great a burden to bear. They would turn her out or return her to her husband regardless of her own wishes."

LaVet pressed her eyes closed, knowing he was right and hating it.

"I have never liked the idea of you leaving the manor without an escort," he admitted quietly.

"I can't expect to have you always at my side."

"Why? When there is no place I would rather be." The boldness with which he said those words made LaVet ache inside. She stared at him, doubting his sincerity.

"Were you scared?" he asked.

"Not until I reached home did it occur to me that I was to be afraid. Of course I should have been frightened… but I kept hearing Barton's instructions in my mind and … and…" Unable to continue, LaVet bit down on her lower lip and again closed her eyes Kenric didn't press her further and LaVet felt a rush of gratitude toward him.

Slipping one hand out from under the lapel of his coat that still hung on her shoulders she reached upward and pressed the palm of her hand to the fingers that still held her face. Relishing the feeling of his touch, LaVet tilted her head slightly, encouraging the contact.

"I feel safe now… here with you, I have always felt safe." She opened her eyes and dared to look up at him. The love that she had discovered for him all that time ago threatened to pour out of her at his closeness.

"I would never harm you." The words floated over her; softly yet firm.

As her eyes met and held his, she knew in a moment of perfect clarity that Kenric was going to kiss her. As the realization hit, and at the same moment she knew that she desperately wished he would do just that.

"Kenric?" Lady Maren called, as she entered the room. "Why has the household been thrown into a tizzy? I can't locate Collingwood or any of the maids." Her sentence stopped abruptly when her eyes fell on the two of them.

"LaVet was met with trouble on the road to Tredan this morning. Collingwood is fetching her some tea and I believe the maids are busy drawing her a warm bath," Kenric answered.

Lady Maren pressed her lips together tightly in a thin frown. "You will catch your death of cold, let's get you out of those wet things." Kenric was forced to move away from her side as Lady Maren fussed her way across the room and, taking LaVet by the arm, led her away.

~ Chapter Fifteen ~

Kenric grabbed the large doorknocker and used more force than was necessary. The sound reverberated through the house. The sounds of scuffling feet reached him just before a timid looking woman answered.

"Lord Leighton."

"Abney-- where is he?" Kenric asked coolly.

"In the drawing room with his daughter and her husband," she answered, wide-eyed. "May I announce your arrival?"

Pushing past her and stepping into the hall he started toward the drawing room. "I need no announcement."

Without ceremony Kenric pushed open the door and strode purposefully into the room. All eyes turned toward him and in an instant Kenric pinpointed the person whom he had come to see.

"Kenric?" Emmaleen whispered, as she and her father stood to receive him.

"To what do we owe this unexpected pleasure?" Lord Abney asked, and gave Kenric a slight bow.

"Abney, I have not come to exchange pleasantries."

"Who the devil are you? I am starting to believe that everyone in this part of the country runs absolutely wild!" The unpleasant looking man who had been lying idly on the sofa sat up enough to give Kenric a disapproving look.

"Lord Ellsworth, this is my father's neighbor, Lord Kenric Leighton," Emmaleen said simply. Ellsworth's eyes grew in size as the realization of who Kenric was hit him and he sputtered something unintelligible.

"What can I do for you, Kenric?" Lord Abney pressed.

"I have come to talk with him." Kenric turned to toward Ellsworth, who had started to go red in the face. "In regards to the incident involving my wife-- I have come to demand recompense."

"Your wife? I didn't know Ellsworth knew Lady Leighton."

"He did not, that is, until their paths crossed this very morning on the road near Tredan. While your... son-in-law was beating his driver to with in an inch of his life, my wife came across them. When she placed herself between *that* man and his driver in an attempt to stop the unnecessary brutality, Ellsworth proceeded to attack my wife." Kenric held his audience captive as he finished.

"Lies! She is a liar!" Ellsworth leaped to his feet, his great face purple with rage.

"You dared to attack a woman, regardless of her status, and then in front of her husband call her a liar, besmirching her reputation?" Lord Abney asked Ellsworth. He waited for the other man to explain himself.

"It... it isn't exactly what happened," Ellsworth said finally, between clenched teeth.

"She did not set you on your back end in a mud puddle then either, I suppose?" Kenric watched as Ellsworth's eyes narrowed.

"It looks as though the lesson in manners I taught her did not stick. I should pass it on to you."

"It is true then? You did indeed attack an unarmed woman on the road to Tredan?" Abney bellowed in disbelief.

"It was hardly an attack, and the impudent female interfered in a matter that was none of her concern." As Ellsworth tried to justify his actions Kenric removed a glove from his pocket and, stepping nearer the man, slapped him hard across the face with it.

"You have insulted my wife for the last time," he growled in a voice that brooked no argument. Kenric dropped the glove at Ellsworth's feet. The challenge was made.

"Tomorrow at dawn, the south field. Bring your sword or, if you prefer, your cane. It won't matter because either way I intend to teach *you* a *lesson*."

Turning sharply he cast a glance at Lord Abney and added, "Make sure he is there," then stormed out of the room.

"Kenric! Kenric!" He recognized Emmaleen's voice but didn't turn around as he descended the stairs toward where his horse stood waiting.

"Please...Kenric..." A hand touched his arm.

"There is nothing you can say." Kenric brushed her fingers off his sleeve then, swinging up into the saddle, glanced down at her. "From now on, you will address me as Lord Leighton. Do not take liberties where none are given." And with that he was gone.

***

The first rays of daylight illuminated the sky as Kenric crested the hill and reined in his horse. Neither talked as the sound of hoof-beats echoed through the still air. Both parties dismounted their horses as they neared the other. Kenric handed the reins to Fitzroy and gave Ellsworth an appraising look.

"I was unsure you would appear."

"It is a matter of pride," Ellsworth sneered, and tossed his reins toward his father-in-law with little care.

"Your pride was never in question; it was your honor." Kenric seethed with anger.

"Gentlemen… isn't there another way to resolve this issue?" Lord Abney called.

"No," both men barked back.

Ellsworth retrieved a thin box from his horse's pack and, opening the lid, tilted it so that the onlookers could see its contents.

"No, dueling pistols will not be necessary." Kenric smirked and tossed a sword at the man who stumbled to catch it in midair. "Let us finish this as it was begun."

Ellsworth glared openly at Kenric then lifted the blade and inspected it. Once he was satisfied he handed it to Lord Abney who also inspected the weapon. When the sword determined to be sound Kenric's too inspected, then each man was searched for hidden daggers or the like.

"To first blood?" Lord Abney asked Kenric. As the challenger it was his choice to say to what end the duel would conclude.

"No-- five… one wound for each insult. The first to deal that number of wounds will be declared the winner. Only then will I be satisfied."

"Five it is. Unless you are pushed to the brink of being physically unable to continue the duel," Ellsworth chortled. It was clear that he felt himself the superior swordsman.

"At your mark." Fitzroy barked. Kenric removed his hat, jacket and waistcoat then loosening his cravat, took up his stance. "Ready… duel!"

Kenric felt confidant that he knew this man's preferred style of swordplay from LaVet's observations of the man, and his propensity for allowing his anger to rule him made it easy for Kenric to formulate a plan of attack.

Anticipating Ellsworth's movements, Kenric took the advantage and easily displaced Ellsworth's first blow with a skilled counter-assault that was timed to perfection to put the other man off his guard.

Ellsworth feinted to one side and Kenric saw his opening before it appeared. Staying in constant motion he lunged forward and like a snake striking pierced Ellsworth's upper arm with the edge of his blade, leaving a red gash in its wake.

Ellsworth swung out violently and made it too easy for Kenric to deflect the blade with the flat edge of his own sword, catching Ellsworth on an unprotected side and leaving another mark.

Like an angry bull the injury only enraged Ellsworth further and he rushed Kenric, who deflected the attack. The two grappled for leverage over each other. This did not last long as Kenric pushed the other man back hard. Ellsworth stumbled, one arm swinging backward widely to regain his balance. This cost him a third hit, to his leg, deeper and longer than the others.

Ellsworth cursed and spat, his brow covered with beads of sweat from the effort the duel was clearly costing him. The fight continued; Kenric moving forward, never giving ground, never yielding, always the aggressor, always ready with a parry or move to elude injury to himself. A clever application of technique coupled with speed and timing earned Kenric a fourth cut; an angry looking gash on the upper jaw.

He eyes measured Ellsworth as the man limped, trails of blood running down his arm, leg and face. It was time to end it.

Kenric thrusted forward, the side of his blade crashing down across Ellsworth's weapon, and watched as the other man's wrist bend backward with the effort of keeping its hold on the hilt. Again, the two blades clashed, then again, until Kenric had weakened him enough that the next solid contact pushed Ellsworth's sword from his grasp

The large man lost his footing and tumbled into the damp grass. "Five," Kenric hissed as the tip of his sword bit into the skin at Ellsworth's shoulder.

"Seems a fitting end… you on your backside in the muck." Kenric twisted the blade ever so slightly before pulling back. "Remember this day, Lord Ellsworth… for I will never forget it… or you."

***

"Hello, girl," LaVet cooed, as she held an apple out to Beauty in the palm of her hand. The white head dipped and smelled the offering then snapped it up greedily.

"Would you care for a brisk early morning ride?" she asked the large brown eyes and patted Beauty on her nose. "Yes? Well good, I've been feeling a bit restless myself."

It didn't take long for LaVet to ready her horse for a ride and she was soon breathing deeply of the bright summer air. They rode at an easy pace for some time before the sight of Fitzroy and Kenric riding toward the stables from the opposite direction caught her attention.

Almost at the same instant she had taken note of them Kenric must have caught sight of her and was moving to intercept.

"You and Fitzroy are out early," she called out, when they came into speaking distance of each other.

"As are you," was Kenric's only reply.

"I felt a bit restless and I don't often have the chance of an early ride." As he drew closer LaVet took note of Kenric's appearance. The lack of jacket, open vest and mussed shirt were all-perplexing.

"Kenric, you are hurt!" she exclaimed, upon examining him further and easily discovering the red stain.

Kenric looked down at his sleeve as if he was noticing the smear of blood for the first time. "No... I am not. It's not mine."

"Not yours? What on earth have you been doing?"

"I had a pressing matter that needed attending to." He didn't look away from her searching gaze.

"A pressing matter... at dawn... that leads you to return with another person's blood on your arm. I thought you said Lord Ellsworth would slink away, tail firmly tucked?"

"He did not issue the challenge," Kenric said simply then rushed on over the top of her protest, "LaVet, I could not allow such an offense to go unanswered."

"Was your vanity so wounded by my actions?" she inquired in hushed tones.

Kenric instantly reached out and took Beauty by the reins, stopping both beasts abruptly. LaVet gasped and looked with wide eyes at him as if she was seeing someone else entirely.

"You know me. Understand me," he said, his voice low and commanding her attention, "You know I have pride... any man worth his salt does... but I am not a vain man. I do not act out of pettiness or perceived injuries."

Feeling ashamed she nodded, "I know."

"Ellsworth's actions demanded satisfaction, because... because you are my *wife*. And that one word holds all the reason I would ever need to teach Ellsworth, or any like him, a well-deserved lesson." LaVet felt the emotion behind each uttered word as it left his lips. In a softer tone he added, "My actions had absolutely nothing to do with the sound thrashing you gave him yesterday. I am not ashamed of you. But I am your husband, and with that comes responsibilities that I have willingly and gladly taken on."

LaVet tore her eyes from his and attempted to regain her composure.

She felt his hand slip under her chin and tilt it upward. "I didn't mean to speak so harshly to you."

"Please don't apologize Kenric. It is my own flaws that blind me."

"Are we friends again?" he asked, with a teasing smile.

LaVet felt her heart fall. "Friends," she muttered painfully.

"Good." He handed her back the reins to Beauty.

She thought for several seconds before bursting out with, "You didn't kill him, did you?"

Kenric laughed, "No... I wanted to. But men like him deserve a lifetime of misery before the welcoming arms of death envelop them. I did however leave him with a few... tokens to remember me by."

"Poor Emmaleen. Whenever I close my eyes I can see her face. She looked a shell of the person I knew. There is no love lost between us, yet I can't help but feel sorry for her now."

"That is where you are the better person, for she has no wish of good to anyone else but herself."

"Did she leave you very heartbroken?" The words had slipped out like water over pebbles and she instantly regretted voicing her thoughts aloud. Gasping, she rushed on, "I'm sorry...I'm absolutely mortified! I don't know why I asked such a question."

"I suppose because you wished to know the answer."

"No," she protested loudly.

Kenric looked down, suppressing a smile. Then taking a deep breath he answered, "You know that the two of us, Emmaleen and I, were thrown into company with each other at a very young age; the only two children in this region from families of great means. I knew as a youth there was talk of a union. There is always talk…" He paused and shifted in his saddle.

"I confess that I fancied myself in love for a time. On the surface Emmaleen can be flawless, but the more I grew to know her the more I saw darkness. When in the company of other women she was kind and thoughtful. She remembered everything about them. Then the moment they were out of her sight she was curt and laughed at their expense, treating everyone as if they were beneath her notice of them.

"It was an unattractive quality, to be sure, but it paled in comparison to how she treated men. Or, more correctly, her many lovers. At times talk is just that, idle gossip, to be dismissed and cast aside. Then there are times when talk is born from truth. I would not repeat what I know if I had not seen it with my own eyes."

"You… saw her with someone else?" LaVet's hand flew to her mouth to stifle her horror.

"A newly engaged man, whose intended soon to be bride was destroyed by their actions."

"Oh my!"

"This particular incident didn't seem to deter her from pursuing me, among others. However, it hadn't even taken me moments after discovering her true nature to realize that there was no way I would have ever loved her-- I didn't even know her. How is it possible to care for someone who doesn't truly exist? She had presented me-- and no doubt many others-- with a fantasy."

"Even so, I still cannot wish a fate as harsh as Lord Ellsworth on anyone."

"You can be sure of one thing, LaVet; she will spend the rest of her life making him equally miserable." He smiled at her.

"I *did* want to know… I have wanted to know since the ball but lacked the courage to ask such a question."

"And are you content with the answer?" Kenric inquired.

"I am sorry that you had to go through that. It could not have been easy to discover that someone you cared about wasn't at all what they seemed," LaVet mused.

"Do not feel sorry for me. My heart is completely safe in the care of another."

~ Chapter Sixteen ~

The May sun was warm and LaVet welcomed its rays as she strolled through the garden paths with Mrs. Long at her side.

"I was sad to learn that the roads had become impassible Tuesday. I was certain some misfortune had befallen you!"

"I do apologize for that."

"Rain such as we have had the past week, I have never seen the like." Mrs. Long closed her eyes and breathed deeply of the air. "Although, this is my favorite time of the year. Winter is washed away and everything becomes green and full of life again. It warms the soul."

"I heartily agree," LaVet commented.

"Oh, I completely let it slip my mind! I have news," Mrs. Long beamed.

"Good news, I hope."

"Lady Emmaleen Abney-- now Lady Ellsworth, I suppose-- has come for a visit! Mr. Long and I were honored by an invitation to dine with Lord Abney and his company just last night."

"Indeed?" LaVet said, with little real interest in the new topic.

"Have you met him?" Mrs. Long pressed.

"Yes, I have met Lord Abney on two occasions now."

"Sir Ellsworth! Oh, how you tease me," she laughed.

"I have," LaVet said simply.

"What did you think of him?" LaVet was saved from having to answer as Mrs. Long did not seem to require a response but rushed headlong into her own assessment of the man.

"I found him to be vastly disagreeable! I have never met with a man of good breeding that was as rude as Sir Ellsworth! I know it is very unchristian to speak of another in such a manner, but truly I was in shock! Also, the amount of spirits he consumed was astonishing and more he drank the worse he became.

"I am mystified as to how a woman as refined and kind as Emmaleen Abney could consent to marry such a horrid man, for I have never been so glad to leave someone's company in my life!"

It wasn't what LaVet had expected to hear, and yet none of it surprised her either.

"I am sorry you found him to be so unpleasant."

"Unpleasant would be too kind a word to describe the encounter. Dear sweet Lady Abney wasn't in the best of spirits either, and there was no after dinner entertainment or game of cards. I can tell you my husband and I felt very slighted by the total lack of hospitality shown or consideration of their guests."

"After all the years of friendship I have enjoyed with Emmaleen I was taken back by her coolness. It seems to me that she is very unhappy in the match and I do wish her father hadn't been so quick to have her married. There were many more gentlemanly suitors that caught her eye in Bath. She could have had one of them instead."

"There are many reasons for marrying. We must not presume to understand every person's motivation for doing so, and perhaps Lady Ellsworth's coolness was due to her being tired after her long journey. The roads could not have been good." LaVet offered an explanation for the perceived rudeness, feeling a strange sort of empathy for Emmaleen and the trials she must face in her marriage to Barnabas.

"Perhaps." Mrs. Long looked thoughtful for several moments. "I suppose that long days on the road mixed with little rest could result in sullen behavior. Yes, I do hope you are right. I would loath to think he behaves in such a manner every day, or that she is truly unhappy."

She thought a moment then added; "I should also take into account the accident Lord Ellsworth was involved in, just Wednesday morning. That would be off-putting for any person."

"Accident?" LaVet asked, interested for the first time.

"Oh, yes! It was much talked of at dinner. You see, Lord Ellsworth was walking with a limp; one arm heavily bandaged and held tightly to his side. There was also an ugly cut on his cheek next to a large bruise. He explained that on an early morning ride his horse had been spooked and bolted. He was thrown and badly injured."

"I see," LaVet said softly. In her heart she knew the truth of the matter and it didn't matter what lies Ellsworth chose to live with. She knew that Kenric believed her, that he knew the truth and had demanded justice in her name. It didn't matter who else ever knew what had really transpired.

Tea was announced and the two took a path leading toward the house. LaVet was pleased that Lady Maren, Frances, Kathryn and Shirleen joined them. It relieved her from having to make conversation.

"Tell me, Frances, are you enjoying your new position?" Mrs. Long asked, stirring a third lump of sugar into her tea.

LaVet heard Frances' positive response but her mind was elsewhere. Her thoughts did not linger long on any topic but strayed back to that of her brother, where they stayed for long painful minutes that stretched into hours.

"My dear, would you direct the maid to bring out more sandwiches? The girls seem to be extra ravenous today." Lady Maren had placed a soft hand on LaVet's arm, bringing her back to the present.

"Of course," she said and excused herself.

"The poor girl. She is still mourning the loss of her brother, I suppose. She does not look well at all. Much too thin, and I can't recall the last time I saw her face alight with happiness. Is there anything I might do to help Lady Maren?" Mrs. Long's conversation wafted behind her as LaVet entered the house. Any responses made by those present would have to remain a mystery to her, for LaVet had no desire to hear her being talked about in hushed tones.

Delivering the message, LaVet didn't feel as though she could make more small talk. Instead, she retreated to Kenric's study and lightly tapped on the door.

"Come." The one word response met LaVet's tentative knock and she pushed open the door to Kenric's study. The sun was setting and darkness shaded in every corner of the large room. The only light was provided by the hearth fire and a few lit candles that illuminated his face as Kenric bent low over a ledger. Catching sight of her, Kenric stood.

"I'm interrupting you. I can return later," she said, starting to back out.

"You are not interrupting anything that does not need interruption. I grow tired of staring at numbers. Please do stay."

With that invitation she closed the door behind her and walked farther into the large space.

"What can I do for you?" he asked, and moved around the table to offer her a chair.

She took it gratefully. "Suddenly I just couldn't stand the idea of going back out to tea. To endure their sad glances in my direction and attempts at conversation that I have no interest in seems too much effort."

"So you came here?" Kenric crossed his arms over his chest.

"I… you don't treat me as though I've been broken," she answered. "I suppose I could have hidden in the library for an hour."

Kenric smiled at this. "Is that what you have been doing in there? Hiding from the rest of the household?"

She heard the hint of humor in his words and a smile touched her lips. "Isn't that what you do in here?"

"Of course. I hate small talk. And don't tell Grandmother, but I have no great love for taking tea with the ladies. Although… you do get all the good cakes and biscuits."

LaVet did smile at this comment with a shake of her head.

"Awe, and there it is," Kenric declared.

"There what is?"

"Your smile. I have missed it these many months."

She looked away from him and clutched at her mother's necklace. "I feel as though I have lost myself, Kenric. I no longer find pleasure in things that once gave great joy," LaVet whispered. "I have been acting dreadfully, like an angry child."

"You have been in mourning for your closest friend and confidant; for your brother," he said softly.

"I have been... I am still," she admitted.

Kenric cleared his throat. "When your mother passed away, you had Barton to lean on, to console each other. Now... he too is gone and you feel lost without him. Is that right?"

She nodded.

"He was a great companion to you, and it was clear that Barton loved you very much. If I may speak freely, I believe you would fare much better if you would talk about it, with a friend who could just listen or give counsel when needed."

"How... when your parents died, how did you... move past the loss?" she asked, with the slightest trembling of her lower lip.

"I confess that for what seemed like a lifetime, I didn't. I was very close to both my mother and father and was devastated by their passing. After some time it was as if a heavy fog lifted. I soon realized that I was not an island in my mourning. Grandmother had also lost them, and I found solace in her company and conversation. We each leaned on the other."

She nodded her understanding.

"LaVet... I am a poor substitute. However, I will always be here... you need not continue to face your grief alone."

Again she nodded, then took a steadying breath. "I must rejoin the ladies before a search party is dispatched." She got to her feet then ventured to meet his eyes.

"Before I go, I wish to say thank you."

"For what?"

"Everything," she answered simply, as the door closed behind her.

~ Chapter Seventeen ~

LaVet was unable to force her feet to move; she felt rooted to the ground beneath her. Kenric placed a tentative hand on her arm.

"Are you ready?" she heard him ask.

"I am not prepared. It is too soon… too soon…" LaVet hesitated for several painful heartbeats. "I don't want to leave him here alone."

The news that her father was now ready to lay her brother's memory to rest with a ceremony for an empty grave had come as a shock to her system. Within hours Kenric had them on the road to Roche Manor, insisting they stay a fortnight to allow all the family ample time to reminisce and then… to say goodbye.

LaVet had grown each day more appreciative of his thoughtfulness as Kenric entertained Octavia's children, counseled with her father, and managed to always be at her side when she might have need of him. He was the very best of men.

Now he seemed to understand that she needed a moment, and lingered near the gate leading to the Roche family cemetery as LaVet moved to stand by her father. Lord Roche stood with his head bent low over his chest; his strong shoulders slumped.

"It's time?" Her father asked.

"Yes, we are ready to leave," she confirmed forlornly.

"And your sister?"

"Octavia is waiting for you at the house with the children to say their farewells."

"I never understood Barton. I never understood you. You and he were so alike, I suppose that's why the two of you bonded so closely as children."

LaVet found it impossible to respond but found it unnecessary as her father went on. "I regret many things in this life, LaVet... and regret is a terrible thing to live with. It eats away at you slowly until there is nothing left. I will always regret not telling your brother how proud I was... how proud I am of the man that he became." His voice cracked with emotion.

"Father..."

"I will regret not telling him those things I assumed he already knew. However, I do not have to live with the same regrets when it comes to you and your sister." Turning to look at his youngest child, he took her hands in his.

"Every man wishes to leave his mark on this earth; to leave a lasting legacy when he passes from this life. When I am gone I will leave behind more than my title, more than a great house, or fortune. I will leave a legacy to be truly proud of-- you and your sister... my grandchildren." LaVet blinked back tears as her father placed a kiss to her brow.

"I am proud of the women you have both become; proud to say that I am your father. You are strong and courageous in ways I could never be. I love you very much, my dear daughter, and my wish for you in this life is to live with no regrets."

"Thank you father." LaVet threw her arms around his neck and hugged him unabashed as she let the tears flow freely. "I love you too."

Holding her at arm's length so that he could look into her face, he continued, "Do not hold in those things that should be shared with those you care about. Do not choose to live with your own regrets. And be happy."

"I will try," she promised.

***

"May I walk with you?" LaVet jumped a little at the sound of Fitzroy's voice behind her.

"Yes please, join me."

"I'm sorry… I didn't mean to frighten you."

"It's quite all right."

"Are you enjoying the warm weather?"

"Pardon my forwardness, but I don't believe you want to take a turn in the gardens with me to chat about the weather," LaVet said, and looked at him from the corner of her eye.

Fitzroy smiled broadly.

"You aren't one for small talk, Lady Leighton, I'll give you that."

"I'll try to be less abrupt in the future," she promised, with a laugh.

"I can see why Kenric is so fond of you."

"Kenric is too kind, for I have many faults," LaVet insisted over Fitzroy's attempts to protest, "Truly, I am not the lady I should be. I have a terrible temper and can be most disagreeable. I also have a penchant for making rash and impulsive judgments; a quality that Kenric has tried to remedy to no avail."

Fitzroy laughed openly at her comments.

"I do believe that Kenric likes you just as you are; faults and all."

"Well, in all truth, I am very difficult. For instance, I had no love for you when we met, and I was unfair in my assumptions that I knew the kind of person you were without getting to know you first," LaVet countered.

Fitzroy looked down and scoffed, "I did not give you any other way to judge my merits when we first met. I was not kind, or gentlemanly. I could offer you a long list of excuses for my poor behavior…"

"Please, it is not necessary. I am living proof that our less pleasant side tends to come out when we have been through… something difficult."

"I do need to ask for your forgiveness. Kenric is a good friend but a horrid secret keeper. I know it was you-- your admonishment of him that brought Kenric to London. Without question you took us into your home in our hour of need. You have borne my insults and treated me and my children with more care than we possibly deserved."

"There is no forgiveness necessary. We both acted foolishly; the past is in the past. Let us move forward as friends," LaVet offered, sincerely.

"I would like that very much," Fitzroy said, truthfully. "I do however have another motive for speaking to you today."

LaVet raised an eyebrow. "You mean mutual forgiveness isn't enough?"

"I'd like to… that is… I have something of great import I must ask you." The atmosphere had changed drastically and Fitzroy looked nervous.

"Of course."

"I'd like your blessing to make an offer of marriage to Frances." As the words left his mouth LaVet felt her legs refuse to move and she stopped short.

"Frances…my blessing… you want to propose?"

"I knew you would be surprised," he smiled.

"That is a very mild term for what I am feeling at the moment. How did this come about? I had no idea you two had formed an attachment." She studied him.

"There is no doubt in my mind that you were fully informed of the details of my last marriage. I can assure you that I have long since lost all tender feelings for the woman who shared my name. So, when I came to live at Leighton Cottage I did so with a heart free of her... not free of anger or mistrust, but of any love I once felt for Valeria."

"I was told about your... wife and so I can understand your anger and mistrust."

Fitzroy looked thoughtful for a long moment, and then a ghost of a smile crossed his face, "At first I fought against everything Frances insisted on doing in regards to the care of the girls. I resented her insistence that I spend time with them each day. Then as the weeks passed, I found I looked forward to my time with Kathryn and Shirleen... as well as my time with Frances.

"Before I knew what had happened I was no longer angry and realized, as I watched Frances laughing with Shirleen and Kathryn that I was, in an odd way, grateful to Valeria for her betrayal. If she had never left me then I would not have attempted to understand or know my own children, or to have been blessed with the chance to be happy once again."

"And are you happy?" LaVet asked, her heart swelling with joy as she watched his countenance change.

Smiling, he nodded. "I am. I have you to thank for that. Your foresight that Frances would benefit my family was... a godsend. The girls do need her in their lives, as I need her in mine. I do not have much to offer her..."

LaVet cut him short. "Your heart is all that she will ever require. Go, ask her right away," she laughed happily.

"Then I have your blessing?" he asked.

"You never needed it."

"You are her friend and she has no family left. I may not need it but I would like it all the same. I know it would mean the world to her."

"Then it is yours!"

Fitzroy beamed at her and pressed a kiss to the back of her hand. "Thank you."

"Go, go!" she urged him. Fitzroy turned and walked at a brisk pace out of the garden. As she stood watching his retreating form she was aware of Kenric appearing beside her.

"I can not remember the last time I saw Fitz looking so pleased. What on earth did you say to him?"

***

"Oh! You've done it again!" Lady Maren huffed in a mocking tone and tossed her cards onto the table. Kathryn laughed with delight.

"You are letting me win," she accused.

"Well, I never!" Lady Maren took out her fan and shielded a smile from the child then, catching sight of LaVet, diverted the attention to her. "Would you honor us with a song?"

"Yes! A song!" Shirleen clapped.

"Might we dance again?" Kathryn bounced in her seat.

"We aren't in the music room. Would this instrument suffice, do you think?" LaVet asked the two in her most serious tone.

The girls both assured her that she could play tolerably well on whatever pianoforte happened to be nearby. She sat to play and the girls interrupted their fathers' conversation so they might have partners.

Soon the room was full of bright merriment and laughter. It was infectious.

"Frances, won't you play a duet with Lady Leighton for us?" Lady Maren implored, "We quite enjoyed your last performance."

Frances moved to sit next to LaVet and they discussed for a moment what song they would attempt to play. Once agreed, music filled the air, followed by their voices as the two women sang. Afterwards they were met with chaos as those assembled clapped and roared for an encore.

Time slipped by at a fast pace and soon the joviality was ended by the lateness of the hour. Frances bid the girls goodnight and promised them faithfully that her removal from the cottage would not last long; just until the wedding could take place in a few weeks-- and that she would indeed see them in the morning. Then, gleaming from head to toe from pure bliss, she exchanged pleasantries with Fitzroy.

"Well, I am going to retire for the night. I must go into Tredan early tomorrow. I have some business at the dressmaker's that can not be put off any longer," Lady Maren was saying as she leaned heavily on her cane.

"Would you like me to go with you?" Kenric asked.

She waved him off. "No, I can very well make it into town and back, unless you have fired your good driver and left me with someone quite incompetent."

"Of course not. You will let me know if you change your mind," he insisted.

Lady Maren stopped and looked up lovingly into his face. "When did the roles reverse? It used to be I that looked after you." She reached up and patted him on the cheek.

"Good night, Grandmother." He smiled after her as Collingwood took her arm and led her from the sitting room.

"You played beautifully tonight," Kenric said, as he turned back to LaVet who still sat in front of the open piano.

"Thank you. It has been a very long time."

"Too long," he agreed. "I was pleased to hear you sing, but more so to hear you laugh."

"I was glad to have a reason to laugh again," she said, with a smile.

"Would you... play for me?" he asked, catching her eyes.

"What would you have me play?" she asked, as a light blush brightened her cheeks.

"Anything." Kenric moved closer to her as if eager to listen.

LaVet thought for a moment then pressed her fingers to the keys. The melody was soft, haunting and beautiful. As the last notes faded she finally dared to look at him.

"Was that... your song? The one you wrote?" Kenric asked, and held out his hand to help her to her feet.

"Yes."

"Thank you for sharing it with me." He gave her a meaningful gaze then added reflectively, "It is good to see a hint of your old self." Kenric smiled at her and taking her fingers gently tucked her hand into the crook of his arm, covered it with his own as he often did. Her free hand moved to cover the necklace at her throat.

"I have never properly thanked you for the return of my mother's necklace, your dealings with Barnabas Ellsworth... your treatment of me and so many other countless things..."

"You never have to thank me; there is no need," he interrupted.

"There is a need," LaVet protested. "Kenric, I wish you to know that your kindness and compassion after the news of Barton's death did not go unnoticed. I know I was not myself," she commented sorrowfully. "I feel as though I am waking from a long sleep," she mused, more to herself than to Kenric.

"That is understandable," he said. "I know all too well that you will never stop missing Barton... There is not a moment that goes by that I do not wish for my father's counsel or my mother's sweet voice. One does not ever really get past the loss of such a cherished loved one. You learn to make it through one day, then the next, and soon the days have turned into years and you are never quite sure how you made it."

Looking at him she understood the depth of his own loss for the first time, and her heart ached with wanting to ease his sorrow. Unable to express all that she was feeling LaVet walked quietly at his side for a few steps before looking up at him again. Only days before he had called her "friend", then hinted at much deeper feelings. Was she the person that held his heart in her care, as he did hers?

LaVet frowned, wondering how many more nights-- how many more days she could continue, saying nothing of what she felt for him. The notion that all the love she held inside her heart would never be expressed was unbearable.

"Kenric, do you think tomorrow will be a particularly warm day?" she asked, as a the solution dawned on her.

"I do not believe so," he answered.

"Do you have any pressing business that needs attention, or could you go out riding with me?" LaVet pressed.

"There is no business so weighty that it cannot wait for a morning ride."

Feeling boldness flood her limbs, LaVet rushed forward. "I thought we could make a day of it; ask cook to pack us a cold lunch and visit the meadow again, perhaps?"

He smiled at her. "I think it a perfect distraction."

***

LaVet breathed in deeply the scent of the trees as Beauty kept pace with Kenric's steed. Summer was in full bloom all around them; the treetop canopies full of thick lush leaves shimmering like jewels in the late morning sunlight.

"Have you ever been to see the wall at Lyme?" Kenric asked, as they slowed to a walk in the narrowing path.

"I have never been to Lyme. My father did take us to the ocean once, but the climate didn't agree with Mother so we never returned."

"Would you be opposed to accompanying me on a trip there?"

She smiled at the thought. "I would like that very much. Do you have business in Lyme?"

Kenric reined in his horse and jumped down, taking both animals reins. "No, no business. I have been feeling for some time that you need a change of scenery, and I can't imagine that Bath in the summer would be your cup of tea."

She laughed, "You are right. Bath at any time of the year is not a place I would care to find myself." The horses now tied, Kenric moved to LaVet and, reaching up, helped her dismount. "Thank you," LaVet murmured as his hands dropped away from her and he made himself busy with retrieving their lunch.

"Then Lyme it is," he smiled, as they started down the narrow path leading to the hidden meadow.

"And when shall we leave?" LaVet pressed.

"That will be up to you." She thought about it for some time.

"It would be best to wait until after Fitzroy and Frances have returned from their honeymoon," she mused.

"In a month, then."

"A month," LaVet agreed, and wasn't able to stop herself from smiling brightly at the prospect.

The remainder of the walk was taken in comfortable silence and soon the smattering of colorful flowers met her gaze, and the sound of a small brook and birdsong filled the air. The meadow was just as she had remembered. LaVet strode into the middle of the blooms, plucking one as she went, twisting the stem between her fingers.

Kenric laid the lunch basket and blanket down and joined LaVet. She felt his presence at her side without having to look at him.

"You look happy," he observed.

Lifting her face to the sun she smiled, "I am." Breathing in deeply she pressed on, "The last time I saw Barton, he told me that I was free... free to make Leighton Manor my prison or my home; that *I* alone had the key to my own happiness. He was right, of course; he was always right." She laughed softly at the memory.

"Your brother was a good man... the best of men. I wish I had been given the chance to know him better," Kenric whispered, with reverence.

LaVet looked directly at him then, her eyes bright with unshed tears, "Kenric," she began, her voice wavering slightly, "My father confided in me that he had many regrets over things left unsaid after the death of my mother... and after Barton's death. He urged me *not* to follow his example. Instead, he encouraged me to say those things that weigh on my mind and live in my heart. So, I thought it would be fitting to come here... to this place, to give you a gift."

"A gift?" Kenric asked, sounding intrigued.

"Yes, it is customary to give a gift on the anniversary of one's wedding." LaVet smiled at him then. "Is it not?"

"Anniversary..." Kenric moved to stand in front of her, looking down into her face with such intensity it caused her heart to race. With the sound of its wild beating pounding in her ears, LaVet mustered the last vestiges of her strength and pressed forward.

"One year ago today we stood in front of God and those we held dear; family and friends, and exchanged vows as strangers. Today, in the sight of God and no one else, I wish to give you the gift of my heart. For it is yours and always has been."

The bloom, now forgotten, slipped from her fingers as Kenric reached out and grasped both her hands tightly.

"LaVet... are you in earnest?" He looked a man possessed, eyes wildly searching her face.

"I love you, Kenric," she breathed. "I hardly know when it overtook me but I have grown to love you so deeply that it can no longer be left undeclared. On this one subject my heart refuses to keep silent."

"There are times when words just stop being necessary..." Kenric's voice was low and each word full of meaning as his gaze moved from her eyes down to her lips then slowly back as LaVet felt a blush deepen the color of her skin.

His hands now cupped her face. Softly his thumbs removed the evidence of tears she had not known were falling. Then slowly, tenderly he drew her to him and his lips claimed hers.

The embrace deepened with unspoken emotion and LaVet found herself clinging to Kenric, her arms wrapped around him, fingertips skimming his jaw, holding his face close; reveling in the feeling of the strength of his arms as she was gathered into them.

Each time the one kiss ended another was eagerly waiting to take its place until LaVet had been so thoroughly kissed that she was unable to stand without assistance.

Trembling, she allowed herself to be drawn in close to Kenric's chest, breathing in the scent of him as her head rested over his heart; its beat echoing hers.

"I fell in love with you, my dearest, loveliest LaVet, a very long time ago. I fear that from my first stumbling across you in the wood I was a lost man." Kenric said next to her hair, his voice low and warm with feeling. "I will accept your gift on the condition that you will continue to hold my heart in your care, for there it has rested for sometime past."

"I had not dared to hope," she laughed, amidst more tears. "I had not dared to dream that you would return my affection."

Again Kenric kissed her. "It is hard to remember a life before you, and I never want to imagine one in which you do not exist at my side."

Catching his gaze she smiled and whispered, "And so you never shall, my love." She then watched in astonishment as the grey tempest died away and the only thing she was able to see shining back from Kenric's gaze... was love.

The End

Loves Journey

Anna Sibbett

2

Authors note

Creating a believable reading experience for a Historic Romance takes investigation on a variety of topics and added details that are not commonplace in today's society.

In preparation for this book, my editing team and I did research on specific sword movements, dueling styles, customs of the time period, style of clothing, modes of transportation, musical instruments, foods commonly eaten, games played during the Regency era and the common U.K. spellings.

If you would also like to learn more about these topics I would suggest these webpages as source material.

http://io9.com/5918644/swordfighting-not-what-you-think-it-is
http://en.wikipedia.org/wiki/Duel
http://www.likesbooks.com/carriages.html
http://www.jasnanorcal.org/ink9.htm
http://www.maggiemayfashions.com/regency.html
http://rth.org.uk/regency-period/family-life/mealtimes
http://www.auroraregency.com/2011/03/etiquette-and-customs-courtship-in.html
http://janeaustensworld.wordpress.com/2008/08/16/games-regency-bucks-played-cribbage/
http://janeaustensworld.wordpress.com/2010/07/12/jane-austen-and-music/
http://grammarist.com/spelling/gray-grey/

About the Author

As a young child B.E. Brown found a love of writing early and began creating worlds on paper as young as 6 years old. It has continued to be a driving force throughout her life. She enjoys working on movie scripts along side her husband, writing skits, plays, short stories, and novels. Brown lives with her husband and two children in Wyoming.

Look for her other books "In the Absence of Light" and "The Love Letters" in

paperback & Kindle edition on Amazon.com

Follow on Twitter B.E. Brown @BEBROWN3 for news on future projects.